# THE BIG WHIZZO

# THE BIG WHIZZO

By David Raine

First published 2018



Published under licence by Brown Dog Books and
The Self-Publishing Partnership, 7 Green Park Station,
Bath BA1 1JB

www.selfpublishingpartnership.co.uk

ISBN printed book: 978-1-78545-279-6
ISBN e-book: 978-1-78545-280-2

Illustrations by Neil Pearson
Editing by Samantha Gardner
Cover design by Kevin Rylands
Internal design by Andrew Easton

Printed and bound by CPI Group (UK) Ltd, Croydon, CR0 4YY

*For the wonders of my life –*
*Amber, Bibi and Felix.*

# FOREWORD

We all enjoy having fun, humans and animals alike. We learn through fun. The scourge of plastic pollution in our oceans, affecting all marine creatures as well as those on land dependent on them as a food source, is far from being a funny subject. But to make the required changes, to change the behaviour of the coming generation, we need to both grab kids' attention and get them to say: "I am going to change my horrid polluting behaviour, I am going to get out there and make a difference – I am GOING TO BE LIKE CAPTAIN JIMMY OCEAN."

It is entirely possible that Horrid Green Custard is not the solution to ocean plastic pollution – but then again, it just might be. Let's read and find out and have fun learning.

David Raine

*This is **Bibi** – she lives in Playing Place Cove, it's boring and lonely there so she dreams of adventure, and WOW does she find it.*

***Princess Liquorice** is absolutely an absolute princess.*

*This is **Captain Jimmy Ocean** - body beach plastic, brain definitely screwball, speech disjointed but also oddly brilliant and magical.*

*This is the **Crab Gang** from Zawn Cove they sing a lot, and a lot and a lot...*

*__Jacob Crab__ is seriously science-ifical for a crab. Added to that he's grown unusually large, crusty and some would say, very ugly. He has seriously powerful claws.*

*Meet **Oscar Shark**, he's a rare Great Right Shark, Captain Jimmy's best mate until he mutates and turns evil.*

# -CHAPTER ONE-

## OLD TOM'S MONSTER CRAB ENCOUNTER

Have you ever dreamt of extraordinary adventures? Have you ever had an extraordinary adventure yourself? An adventure that was so wild, so amazing, so beyond anything that you ever thought possible, an adventure that was on the very edge of your control and, at times, possibly even beyond it?

This story is such an adventure.

And this adventure is not simply an adventure for its own sake, for the pure fun of having it, for the sheer amazement of being totally and blown away crazy – it is an adventure that has meaning, an adventure that has the power to change, to alter the very world, our planet, our oceans for the better.

Now that really is an adventure!

Bibi did not at first realise that she had special powers. Special powers are not like Christmas presents that arrive

all neatly packaged and ready. Special powers become realised over a period of time; special powers have to be unwrapped slowly to give them space and time to grow and to become amazing.

Bibi Lopez-Miller unwraps her special powers slowly throughout this adventure, and others still in the making – they are her gift. But in the very beginning she has absolutely no idea that they exist at all.

*But then, isn't that what having an adventure is all about – discovering the unknown? However weird or scary that might be?*

Bibi Lopez-Miller was just eleven years old at the start of the adventure and was quite different to other girls of her age. Her mother, Elspeth, was Spanish and a well-known marine biologist. Her father was English and a wildlife photographer, and that was why Bibi's name was Lopez-Miller: Spanish Lopez and English Miller.

Bibi loved being both Spanish and English except, that is, for her two Spanish cousins who lived in Valencia. That, at times, could be a massive pain – for one thing, they were really mad about computer games and that was one thing that Bibi had come to be really bored with: *'there's a world beyond screens,'* she'd tell them, but they never listened.

Bibi was a girl who very much enjoyed her own imagination and creating her own imaginary worlds. Like her dad she was very visually aware, and like her mum she was super curious. It was partly because her mother recognised that she was a little bit special, and partly because the local country school '*was not up to your high standard*,' as her mum said, that ever since they had moved from the city to the country Bibi had been taught at home by her mum.

In the beginning, Bibi had hated the idea of moving. It meant leaving the school that she loved and all of her city friends, and, particularly, the fact she was moving to a small fishing village in a very isolated part of the coast was the pits, at least in the beginning. But as the months passed she grew first to sort of accept, and then to quite like, and (the biggest surprise of all to her) almost start to love Playing Place Cove, as the tiny village was called. She loved the open space of the country and particularly the vast, open ocean space where her imagination could float around just as it wanted to. And she even got to like the grumpy old people who lived there, and the grumpy old people got to like her.

For the grumpy old people, Bibi Lopez-Miller was the breath of fresh air that had been long missing in their lives and, perhaps because of this, they embraced her and in a funny way she quickly became the 'daughter of the village'.

When she ran or cycled or skateboarded by, they would call out, 'Morning, Bibi. Has Princess Liquorice caught any rabbits this morning?'

And Bibi would call back, 'Not yet, but she will, she never gives up trying. How are your potatoes coming on?'

'Very nicely. Really early this year. Pop by tomorrow and I'll give you some for your mum.'

'Thanks, I will. Bye Mrs Bramble. Off on an adventure.'

'Oh! How exciting. Good luck. Bye.'

Princess Liquorice, or Liqcs as Bibi often called her, was Bibi's black, wire-haired, feisty, funny and very, very smart terrier dog. Princess Liquorice had so many rabbits to chase that Bibi joked the rabbits needed to book chasing appointments.

The main reason that they had moved to the coast was because Mum Elspeth was writing a book. The book was called 'Our Oceans Are Dying', and it was about the problem of ocean plastic pollution. In their new house, her mum's study looked out over the Atlantic Ocean and that, she said, gave her amazing inspiration.

Bibi kept a secret diary; in it she wrote about imagined adventures and sea monsters. She sometimes wrote her diary in code and sometimes in very, very small writing that could only be read with her *magic* magnifying glass. Her *magic* magnifying glass was given to her by her fisherman friend, Old Tom. It was made of well-worn brass and the lens was a bit scratched.

In her imagination, Bibi half-believed that her mother had a way to communicate with sea monsters. How, she was not sure, but if her suspicions were true, then she was determined to get to the bottom of it. Bibi's mother was very hard working, always reading books or working on her computer doing emailing and boring stuff like that.

There were some days when Bibi even imagined that the computer screen was her mother's magic connection to the sea monster world.... A sort of very mysterious, if not magic, portal. But then, that was just too much wild imagination... Wasn't it? *Wasn't it*?

Being a wildlife photographer meant that Bibi's dad, Frank, spent months away working on assignments.

*'Assignment'* was a word, said softly and stretched out, or whispered in Princess Liquorice's ear, which she said when she was a bit sad or lonely. To her, it sort of sounded like a comforting word – a sort of teddy-hugging word or a daddy-hugging word.

Bibi missed her dad a lot and compensated by dreaming her own dreams and creating her own mind world.

**'Assssignnnmennt.'**

One particular morning in early spring, Bibi woke feeling almost as if she was a different person. The day was bright and clear of sea mist and the ends of her fingers tingled a bit, but she could not exactly pin down a reason for that, except that perhaps she had been sleeping awkwardly.

She was up to date with the home schooling work, the previous day had been wet and windy so she had done extra then, so this was a free day, a day for doing exactly what she wanted to do.

If you didn't have a vivid imagination, then the fishing village of Playing Place Cove could be extremely boring – awesomely boring even. Awesomely this and awesomely that was how Bibi described most things, even her blonde hair, that her mum had platted that morning, she described as awesome when she looked at it in the mirror.

'You're so pretty, even more so this morning,' her mum had said kissing her. To which Bibi replied: 'Awesome!' and Princess Liquorice had barked, 'Slim and pretty, and pretty and slim, just awesome my *lovely*.'

Luckily Bibi was the only person who could understand Princess Liquorice. In fact, mysteriously and magically she could understand absolutely everything that Liqcs said which made them very close friends, very close friends indeed.

Straight after breakfast they ran together down to the harbour, Princess Liquorice barked wildly, jumped and ran excitedly in circles in the narrow, cobbled streets of Playing Place Cove.

Princess Liquorice was feeling particularly delighted because she now had the strange, obviously infectious, tingly feeling running all the way though her black wiry fur and up her waggy tail, and that tingly feeling was saying to her – 'big adventure, big adventure, big adventure.'

'Is that dog dangerous?' postman ('Moans-a-Lot'), as Bibi had named him, called out as he nervously cycled past.

'She eats postmen!' Bibi called back darting into a side alley short cut with Liqcs racing along behind.

Whizzing over the smooth cobbles, past the pub that was closed, the shop that only opened mornings; Bibi zipped in through the ringing bell door of Granny Bluebell's café and cake shop on the ground floor of a deserted hotel, grabbed a sticky bun and a sausage roll, put £1.65 on the glass counter and zipped out again.

She sat on the harbour wall, feet dangling over the water and ate the bun while Princess Liqcs gobbled down the sausage roll in just three gobbly bites.

Playing Place Cove harbour was small and old with just two fishing boats, *Amazing Mary* and *Morning Star*, bobbing at their moorings.

The third fishing boat that belonged in the harbour, Old Tom's dilapidated craft aptly called, *Still Afloat*, appeared motoring in around the old stone jetty having been out on a fishing trip. Bibi waved, Princess Liquorices barked. Old Tom the fisherman was her only real friend in Playing Place Cove.

Old Tom talked to crabs. He had given her his great grandfather's magic magnifying glass with the bent brass handle. She believed that Old Tom knew about things, monsters and things. Often, he moaned about how things were different when he was a lad, how there was, 'none of that there plastic and stuff floating about, messing the place up, killing birds and fish and the like... and 'aving a weird effect on me crabs and lobsters. Awful it is how people don't care no more 'bout throwing stuff down. Fishes eat it, plastic gets in 'em, then we eat the fish and we'm eating plasticky bits too. How daft can people get, that's what I'm asking myself.'

When they went out on fishing trips together and lifted crab pots that he had scattered all along the coast, Bibi liked to hear him say things like: 'C'mon my handsome,' and 'you're a good'un, let's be 'aving yuh my lovely.'

Hidden among the pile of crab pots on the quay, Bibi had a bucket, some line and a few old bits of bacon rind. She collected them, tied a piece of rind to the end of the line and dangled it over the wall into the water to catch crabs while she waited for Old Tom to motor slowly in. The *Still Afloat's* engine was old, smoky and slow.

Almost immediately when she dropped the bacon rind attached to the line into the water there was a great tug, very nearly pulling her off the wall and into the harbour. She yanked the line up, no crab - and the rind had been eaten in one piece. 'Wow! That must have been a MONSTER crab,' she gasped.

Old Tom spotted Bibi and Princess Liquorice on the harbour wall and started waving and shouting. That's very odd, Bibi thought, and said to Princess Liquorice, 'Old Tom rarely says anything much, particularly to humans, and he never waves, and he certainly never waves excitedly. Something very weird has happened to him – is he infected with the tingly feeling too? This day is getting awesomely exciting.'

'Woof, woof,' Princess Liquorice agreed.

As he pulled alongside the harbour wall, he threw a rope ashore for her to catch and shouted up, 'Them blighters crushed mi pots and escaped. Huge, they'm be... HUGE. That's what's they is. Never seen the like. Claws big enough to crush the *Still Afloat* to matchwood. Never in all my days has I seen killer crabs on steroid-icles like they is.'

'What you need, Old Tom, is a sticky bun. Shall I get you one, and a brew?' Bibi offered, seeing how shaken Old

Tom was by his terrifying experience, and knowing how he loved sticky buns and a good strong cup of tea.

'Aye, that's a good plan. Tell Granny Bluebell to put it on my tab, an' get one fur yerself and a sausage roll for the doggie.'

Bibi was quickly back, and they all sat on a stone seat with tea, sticky buns and a sausage roll, their backs to the wall, sheltered from the wind and looking out to sea.

'It was never like it in my father's day,' Old Tom said after a lot of slurping and thinking. 'Things is 'appening, strange things is 'appening... Pots smashed to smithereens and the like. It's the plastic pollution in the oceans that's doing it, mark my words.'

Bibi whispered into Princess Liquorice's ear, 'I've got a plan. We need to collect supplies.'

'An ADVENTURE?' Liqcs growled very quietly, realising it was a very secret thing.

'Could be the biggest you've ever been on,' Bibi whispered back. Princess Liquorice's eyes glistened with excitement. How she just loved real adventures!

Bibi sent a quick text to her dad, which read:

*'Have you ever photographed monster crabs? Big kiss from me and a big lick from Liqcs. X'*

Her dad replied almost immediately from somewhere hot and dusty in middle of Africa:

'Have you been eating too many sticky buns and imagining monsters again? X'

'Too many buns, yes,' she replied, 'imagining things, no, no, no!'

'Get a photo of this MONSTER, send it, and I'll believe you.'

'THAT'S THE PLAN, Daddy-kins. Awesome adventure on the way, watch out for updates.'

Bibi immediately sent the message back.

She scrambled over the back wall of their cottage, climbed the pink flowering cherry tree to her open bedroom window and then lowered a rope with a basket attached for Princess Liquorice to jump into and be hauled up. Liqcs knew the routine, as they often snuck in and out of the cottage that way especially when they were on secret missions. But this time, twisting and wriggling with excitement, Princess Liquorice very nearly fell out.

Struggling not to bark, yelp or growl was very nearly a total impossibility.

'Make sure that you don't make a sound,' Bibi instructed Princess Liquorice again. 'It's one thing Dad knowing that we have an awesome PLAN – he's in wild and hot Africa – but Mum will want to know details and all sorts of rubbishy things like where are you going and don't be back late and be careful, and all of that mum stuff.'

When she had first arrived in Playing Place Cove, Bibi had not immediately understood how different she was to the friends whom she had left behind in the city. In the city she had not had the same opportunities to play outside on her own because the city had dangers that did not exist in Playing Place Cove. Not dangers from possible nasty people, though. In Playing Place Cove the dangers were more physical, like getting cut off by the tide or falling off the cliff. Lots of the people there were retired, grew vegetables and looked out for their neighbours. They looked out for Bibi too, she knew that, her mum knew it, and she felt safe, safe to spend time on dreams and adventures.

And there was another difference between her, her city friends and her Spanish cousins that had become more pronounced since she had lived by the sea. She had almost entirely lost interest in screens: computers, iPads and gaming on her smartphone.

Mum Elspeth had been brought up in a small Spanish village on the Mediterranean coast where everyone knew everyone, and as a child she had played day and night outside in the street or on the beach. To her, the new outdoor exploring life that Bibi now had in Playing Place Cove was the life that was normal to her, and she felt the more natural life, the more wholesome, the more character-developing life.

Bibi knew that she had more freedom that any of her old friends would dare to imagine was possible.

Was it a good thing or was it bad? One thing was sure, it allowed masses of space for adventures.

Bibi put a torch, some binoculars, a camera, her smartphone and her magic magnifying glass into her backpack.

Before climbing back down the garden tree, she tiptoed past her mum, working on her computer, raided the fridge for herself and collected biscuits, water and other '*special*' supplies for Princess Liquorice.

As Bibi very quietly slid her bedroom window shut, she noticed a photo of her Spanish cousins on the windowsill and it gave her a deliciously mean idea.

The previous Christmas, Bibi's cousins, Maria (7) and Immaculada (11), had been to stay in the cottage. They found Playing Place Cove cold, wet and very boring, and never stopped telling Bibi how warm and sunny Valencia was.

'So,' Bibi said to herself as she slithered down the tree, 'this will show them that *warm and sunny* can be awesomely boring too when compared with — She started texting furiously:

'Off on adventure mission/assignment into the world of monstrously large sea creatures. Will update later. Love from Bibi & Ligcs.'

Bibi wrote her text in Spanish so that the cousins fully understood that Playing Place Cove had a more exciting edge than they might have realised, and, very importantly, none of the adventure and excitement of the message was lost in translation. She also added loads of grinning emojis to her message to add to the '*so there*' effect.

# - CHAPTER TWO -

## FLYING BOOTS AND A MAGIC COLLAR

Bibi and Princess Liquorice ran south along the narrow cliff path. The sky was clear with only distant clouds along the horizon, although the sun was getting higher and there was a gentle cooling breeze blowing in from the sea.

But running and occasionally doing the odd summersault, Bibi was soon feeling hot. She stopped and removed her sweatshirt so that she was only wearing a T-shirt, shorts and trainers, stuffed it into her backpack and continued on.

Princess Liquorice constantly yelping with excitement, and sometimes doing her yelping war cry, dashed back and forth at very high speeds, sniffing for rabbits and any other sniffy smells that might be interesting among the sea grass, patches of bramble and early summer flowers.

They were both very, very excited.

The first part of Bibi's plan was to head for Old

Chapel Lookout Tower, the tower that Playing Place Cove residents said was haunted and where Postman Moans-a-Lot was always threatening to send Princess Liquorice when she barked at him.

In the minds of all the villagers, it was a scary place. Only two days before, Granny Bluebell from the village shop had whispered to Bibi, as she was putting her £1.65 down on the glass counter, that a mysterious light had been spotted there in the dead of night; a glimmering light, like a swinging lantern light; a sort of coming and going light.

'Never go there, girl, not even in the light of day,' Granny Bluebell had warned. 'Things happen around these parts that are not rightly understood.'

But Old Chapel Lookout Tower looked down on the very spot that Old Tom had his lobster and crab pots among seaweed-covered rocky outcrops. Despite Granny Bluebell's dire warnings, it seemed to explorer/adventurer/soon-to-be MONSTER crab discoverer and photographer, Bibi Lopez-Miller, the perfect spot to spot *grotesquely grown marine enormities*, when the tide was low and the rocky, seaweed-covered outcrops were fully exposed.

Old Tom's words still rang in Bibi's ears and made her tingle with excitement – *'HUGE that's what's they is. Never seen the like, claws big enough to crush the Still Afloat to matchwood. Never in all my days have I seen killer crabs on steroid-icles.'*

Princess Liquorice ran into the ruin of The Old Chapel Lookout Tower, jumped up onto a pile of fallen stones in one corner and scratched like crazy at an old piece of canvas partly hidden by the stones.

Princess Liquorice's sixth doggie-sense was almost like a magical power, and Bibi believed in it utterly and completely. She had the power to just *know* things; Bibi often thought this to herself or wrote about it in her secret diary in very, very small writing – that could only be read by a magic magnifying glass.

But what she discovered this time was truly and utterly and awesomely and really beyond-description, amazing.

'Boots,' gasped Bibi. 'Wow! And what boots they are! Just look at them,' she said, turning them round and round, looking inside, feeling the strange texture inside and out.

'*Magic* boots?' growled Princess Liquorice in a low, quite awe-struck growl. 'Real magic boots, aren't they? Have you ever seen magic boots before? I think that they're almost a bit scary. Why don't you see if they fit? What do you think they were doing here? Is this part of the adventure, do you think?'

Princess Liquorice gave them a good sniffing. They seemed okay, sort of passed the initial sniff test, but still she was very wary of them.

Bibi sat on a rock, removed one of her trainers and

cautiously slipped her foot into the left boot. On the outside, the 'magic' boot looked oversized but mysteriously it fitted. It fitted perfectly. More than perfectly. It fitted in such a good fitting way that it gave Bibi the feeling that she never wanted to take it off. She put the right boot on and stood up. Standing up they felt even more comfortable; they almost felt like a 'comfort trap,' if such a thing as a 'comfort trap' really existed.

'They are amazingly comfortable,' she purred, wiggling around a bit.

'Made for you, made especially for you. Is it a trick? A trap? What does it mean? Why were they hidden there? They weren't here the day before yesterday: we were here then and I'd have sniffed them out if they had been here. Maybe you should take them off. I'm getting a spooky doggie feeling about them. What if they are so comfortable that you never ever want to take them off? I mean, could you have a shower in them? And having a bath would be terrible. And I could never sleep on the bed without being kicked off by enormous great boots.'

'Stop worrying,' Bibi laughed. 'They're just boots. Someone must have left them here. Perhaps they're circus boots, perhaps someone was here practising circus tricks and left them to come back and practise another day.

'But look at them. What is this they're made from?

Strange silver scales, like large luminescent fish scales? And look, there's a sort of lens in the back of the boot just above the heel. Lift one up and let me look underneath,' Princess Liquorice said, sniffing every detail intently. 'Ugh! What's that?' Princess Liquorice jumped back.

'What is it?' Bibi lifted a foot and twisted around to look at the sole. 'Well that is weird,' she had to admit. There was a small orange pad.

She tentatively touched it. 'It has a sort of pulse,' she said, not feeling at all fearful or feeling at all inclined to take her finger away.

Bibi took a couple of steps out through the stone arch that had once been the Lookout Tower doorway. 'They are amazing to walk in. They look clumpy but they sort of almost float – it's both weird and lovely walking in them, just a very floaty sensation.' She walked out further onto the grass, Princess Liquorice scampering along beside her. 'Look, there's a pink button sort of thingy on the ankle,' Princess Liquorice barked, examining the slight protruding button very closely.

'They feel magically electric,' Bibi said. 'Now I'm getting a tingling sensation all over my skin. It's the weirdest thing! I bet Granny Bluebell would be shrieking and running for her life if she were here,' Bibi laughed taking a few more steps and skipping a bit. 'Maybe the boots glow in the dark and it was glowing boots, not a lantern, that the Playing Place Cove villagers saw. Or, are they phantom boots, boots that in the night are worn by a ghost, a scary spirit thingy that flickers with light?' teased Princess Liquorice, partly light heartedly and partly concerned that something was about to go very wrong.

'Doesn't bother me, today they are mine – awesome adventure coming up.' Bibi was more interested in trying to do some skippy-dance steps, because her legs just felt like skippy legs with the magic boots on.

'Well what if, what if, what if the magic boots belong to a really, really angry ghost, a ghost who does mean and nasty things to people who use the ghost boots?'

'OH NO! Is that possible? Brilliant! How awesome would that be?'

Princess Liquorice was still feeling concerned, and her doggie senses were telling her that there was something very peculiar about the boots, something dangerous even. She was still giving them some very close scrutiny sniffing when her nose very lightly touched the pink protruding button on the ankle.

'Oh no! Oh wow! Oh YES!' Bibi yelled as she slightly rose into the air, no more than 30 centimetres, but still she was up clear of the grass and flowers, in the air, just hovering in the air. Not resting on grass stems or anything like that, but really and truly hovering in clear, clean, ozone-rich, fresh air. Thin air that balloons can float up in, but never human eleven-year-old girls wearing boots, shorts, a T-shirt and a baseball cap. NEVER EVER!

'Come down, take them off. I knew it. They're ghost boots. A ghost left them here – it's obvious, ghosts hover, so ghosts need hovering boots. Get them off – they could be really dangerous.

What if you become a ghost?' Princess Liquorice was barking madly while running round and round in circles.

'OMD,' Bibi cried. 'Oh my dog, look at me. I can fly, fly, fly, fly in the sky, fly high. And you know what? I can turn just by thinking about turning, go up and down by thinking, OMD... It's fantastic!'

Princess Liquorice was neither listening nor watching. Princess Liquorice had had an idea. Maybe it was a doggie-inspired, doggie-intuitive idea, or maybe it was that she had put two and two together and figured something out. It didn't matter because the result turned out to be the same remarkable thing.

Bibi was still flying around saying, 'So what if they do belong to a mermaid ghost, so what if they do? Mum always says it's good to share and I think that that is absolutely very true. Sharing with a mermaid ghost – how about that! Wow-zzzeey, wow!' She was talking to herself because

Princess Liquorice had disappeared back into the Lookout Tower.

Bibi was still hovering around getting used to the mind control mechanism that appeared to operate the magic flying boots when Princess Liquorice emerged from the tower with a collar in her mouth. She dropped it at Bibi's feet.

'Ha ha!' she barked, scratching the ground in mad excitement. 'See this, see what I've got, bet it's better than yours.'

'What have you found? Where was it? Oh, it's a collar. It's quite pretty, isn't it – blue shell studded, that's nice. We should put it on the wall. Some dog must have pulled it off. The owner will be looking for it,' Bibi said and flew off.

Princess Liquorice angrily picked it up, ran off to where Bibi was hovering over a patch of sea-pink flowers and dropped it again.

'Put it on,' she demanded, growling her meanest, nastiest growl. 'Put it on me, and put it on now.'

'You can't just take things. It belongs to another dog,' Bibi protested.

'Okay,' Princess Liquorice smiled, in a way which said you really don't know what you're on about, and she continued. 'Let's say I'd just like to try it on to see how it looks and after you can put it on the wall.'

'Oh okay,' Bibi agreed, 'but don't think that you're keeping it.'

To keep Princess Liquorice happy, or at least not complaining, Bibi clipped it on and immediately flew off. She was a bit annoyed. Liqcs had a very insistent terrier side to her nature that sometimes really got on her nerves.

A few seconds later, Princess Liquorice was pulling Bibi's plait. She was pulling her plait with her teeth. She was right behind her tugging at her plait and growling a deep, meaningful growl.

'What is that?' Bibi turned snappishly. 'OMD! No you're not, no, this is crazy, I don't believe it... You're flying... You're flying too!'

'You see, you see, you see... Didn't believe me,' Princess Liquorice yelped madly as she zoomed off.

Not being a dog for doing simple flying, she did a wacky backflip, a loop-the-loop twice, the second time with her tail wagging super-fast wags, and then zoomed out over the cliff, disappearing from sight before reappearing barking her head off with totally manic excitement.

'That's just showing off,' Bibi laughed, flying up to meet her so she could rub her tummy.

'Princesses are known for showing off,' Liqcs barked back, coughing and growling and almost choking while whizzing off into a fast barrel roll. 'Bowee!' she barked wildly.

'Let's land and think about things for a moment,' Bibi suggested, catching up with her again. 'This adventure day has suddenly become absolutely more than just a bit crazy. We need a pause, to get our breath and try to work out just what is happening... Flying boots and flying collars are definitely not everyday things... Something very weird is happening here.'

They landed on a soft grassy bank close to the cliff edge and looked down over the seaweed-covered rock outcrops below that were becoming more and more exposed as the tide receded.

'Who could have left them there? The boots and collar, I mean,' Bibi pondered aloud, taking a drink of water from her bottle and pouring some into a small bowl that she kept in her backpack for Princess Liquorice. 'I mean, there are adventures and there are adventures, and we've never had one this weird. I mean, are we in the middle of a dream or something? I know that Granny Bluebell warned us about strange happenings but, well, this flying business is just beyond strange.'

'Does it matter? It's fun and that's what really matters. So, let's just have fun, then put the collar and boots back where we found them, go back and have lunch, and then come back later and see if they're still there,' Princess Liquorice suggested, clearly eager to zoom off again.

'What will that prove?' Bibi asked, biting into an apple and giving Liqcs some cheesy snacks.

'Well, if it's a dream or not, dreams don't last that long... Well not until after lunch they don't,' Princess Liquorice growled between crunches.

'Okay, we'll do that. But first I just want to try something else. Remember what we're here for; we're here to spot giant crabs, the ones that have been crushing Old Tom's crab pots. Spot them and get photos to send to Dad and the cousins.'

Look, there are two of them there,' Bibi pointed out beyond the rocks, further out, where waves were breaking. See those black flags on sticks? Those are Old Tom's pot markers. So, what I thought we could try, but we do have to be careful and sensible, remember what I promised Mum – always to be very, very careful when near the sea – and that is because...? Bibi poked Princess Liquorice for a response.

'Because the sea is very dangerous,' Princess Liquorice responded with the enthusiasm of a soggy-bottomed bread pudding.

'That's right. Glad that you're taking this seriously and not just thinking about zooming around flying,' Bibi gave her a hug but Princess Liquorice wriggled away.

'What I want to try and do is to fly out over the rock outcrops to search for giant crabs. Before we got this sort of weird, magic or whatever it is, flying opportunity, I was planning to wade out at low tide. But if we fly in carefully and slowly we'll have more chance of surprising them before they scuttle back and hide in the seaweed. So that's the plan. But what are we going to be?' Bibi prodded Princess Liquorice in the ribs.

'We are going to be super careful because the sea is very dangerous and people and dogs easily get drowned or cut off when the tide comes in or knocked over by big waves and get their mouths full of salty water, which is nasty to drink, and...' Princess Liquorice whined on.

'Okay, okay. You don't need to do your lifeguard public service message thing. But remember, it is serious. Just think, if the helicopter had to come and rescue us, how would we explain that '*we were just doing a wee bit of magic boot and collar flying out over the rocks, mister pilot, Sir.*'

'I'd say, I bet I can fly faster than you Mr Pilot. Race yuh,' Princess Liquorice replied, taking off, hovering and crouching into a starting position.

'Can you stop larking about, even for a second? We are going to be very careful. We are not going to fly over water where we will be out of our depth. Have you got that?' Bibi instructed, firmly.

'Yes, Bibi ma'am.'

'Okay then. Let's go. No zooming around mind,

especially while going down the path to the beach, it's steep and we have absolutely no idea how these things work or if the batteries, if they have batteries, will suddenly just die on us,' Bibi grabbed Princess Liquorice by the hair on the back of her neck and looked her hard in the eyes. 'Are you listening?'

'Grrrrr,' was the only reply she got.

Halfway down the cliff path there was a large overhang of rocks that blocked the view of the beach below and the lower part of the narrow path. It was not until they were nearly at the overhang that they heard voices from people coming up.

'Quick! Sit down, sit down here on the edge of the path and we'll pretend that we're resting and looking at the view... If they see us flying, they'll probably... well they'll probably either fall off the cliff or run back to the beach tearing their hair out. Sit down, sit down.' Bibi pulled Princess Liquorice in beside her and sat there stroking her while attempting to make her own smile look less forced.

The couple came into view. They had a Dalmatian dog with them. The dog was out ahead and the couple were moving slowly up the steep incline.

'Remember, no messing around,' Bibi whispered. 'Act normal...' and then added, whispering right into Princess Liquorice's ear, 'if normal is ever possible for you.'

Princess tensed up; the hair on her back stood up and she growled low and threateningly deep down in her throat.

Bibi picked a few flowers. The dog and the couple continued to climb towards them. Princess Liquorice continued her low growling but they went straight past.

They passed within inches of where Bibi and Princess Liquorice were sitting without turning their heads, even though Bibi said, 'Hello, lovely day.' And the Dalmatian did not turn even the slightest bit to sniff Princess Liquorice who was, for the very first time in her life, completely gobsmacked.

'We're invisible. Did you see that? We're invisible.' Bibi was incredulous.

'Not just invisible, but sniff-isible too,' Princess Liquorice whispered as if although they were invisible and sniff-isible they might not be sound-isible.

Without saying anything more, Princess Liquorice flew off back up the path. She flew round and round the two hikers, under the Dalmatian's tummy, sat for a while on its back and then returned to Bibi who was still sitting scratching her head.

# - CHAPTER THREE -

## THE CAVE THAT WAS NEVER THERE BEFORE

In a bit of a state of shock and feeling a little bit fearful, Bibi and Princess Liquorice glided down to the small rocky beach at Zawn Cove without speaking. It was as if flying was one thing, but being invisible was something a whole lot different. Being invisible was scary, very scary. What was going to happen next, Bibi was nervously wondering, and what if it lasted and they were still invisible when they got home? Had Granny Bluebell been right? Did things '*as can't be explained*' really happen?

Zawn Cove beach was somewhere where they played most days – particularly when the tide was out, because there were lots of rockpools – but not the day before because it had been raining.

When the tide was out there was a lot of white sand between ridges of rocks, which had limpets and mussels attached to them by the thousands. Sometimes Bibi collected shells there – it was a good place for all sorts of shells. Sometimes she collected pieces of driftwood to take home to add to her 'driftwood garden creation'. Sometimes she played there with Lucy and Tom, the children from a nearby farm, and they would fish with nets in the rock pools or play touch or hide and seek in around the rocks.

Today, Zawn Cove was different. Today, Zawn Cove had totally changed. Today, Zawn Cove had a cave that was never there before. Today, Zawn Cove had a small wooden jetty that was never there before, and tied up to the jetty was a very peculiar, a very peculiar indeed, sailing boat. The sailing boat looked as if it was made almost entirely from bits of beach plastic, the sort of rubbish plastic and other bits, like canvas and rope and bottles, that get washed up by the tide.

Bibi cautiously put a foot on the sand: it left a print. She had rather feared that not a mark would be left and that being invisible meant that footprints did not show either.

No one was to be seen; no one was on the sailing boat, no one in sight at all. One thought that flashed through Bibi's mind was that perhaps they were not actually invisible at all but that the two people and the Dalmatian dog had been some sort of strange optical illusion. Had both Bibi and Princess Liquorice just imagined them?

It was getting more and more curious by the minute.

'What's that horrible smell?' barked Princess Liquorice, sniffing the air frantically. 'It's coming from the cave, that cave over there, that cave *that was never there before*. Ugh, it's really foul!'

Bibi hovered out along the jetty and looked down into the sailing boat. It was as she first thought. It was made from thousands of bits of plastic bits: old broken sand buckets, plastic fizzy-drink bottles – all made of plastic that could be carelessly thrown away and then washed back up on the beach somewhere. All of the plastic bits were encased in a clear substance that bound them together and formed the boat shape.

It was called *Ocean Flyer*. The name was painted on the stern in a very strange flowery writing script, which only added to the deep mystery.

It was like nothing that she had seen before. It was nothing like Old Tom's boat; his boat was solidly built and painted blue and white. Anyway, this sailing boat was more than twice as big as his fishing boat and had a towering mast that curved backwards. Bending down, she touched it very cautiously. There was just something very odd about it that worried her. It was not just the fact that it was here and had not been here before; it had, as she described it to herself in her thoughts, an aura, an aura of deep mystery, an aura of other worldliness, a disturbing but at the same time a mesmerisingly exciting aura.

With the very tip of her finger, she touched the high curving bow, the stem post that had old deflated balloons, bottle caps and loads of bits of coloured rope cast into it – it felt like nothing that she had ever felt before – it felt like...

Princess Liquorice barked her really-worried-about-something bark. Bibi looked up. She was some way off near the cave entrance. Bibi zoomed over. Stinking green smoke was pouring out of the cave, and because of the smoke and because of the general dimness inside it was not possible to see beyond the billowing smoke.

'What's up?' Bibi asked, landing on the spongy sea grass.

'There's someone in there, I heard something.' Princess Liquorice was crouched right down peering and sniffing beneath the smoke.

'Perhaps they're trapped. Wow! That is a seriously foul stink. Maybe there was a rockfall and that's why there's now a cave where before there wasn't a cave,' Bibi surmised, holding her hand over her mouth and nose and trying to peer into the gloom. 'Can't see anything. Can you hear anything?'

'No, but someone's in there. Believe me, I know. Dogs know,' Princess Liquorice flew up to look in from higher up, but the smoke was even thicker and she could see nothing.

'I definitely think that there's been a rockfall. It must be an old mine working that collapsed, and all of this stinky smoke was trapped inside and now it's escaping. Let's get back; breathing it in could be dangerous. It could be poisonous, it certainly stinks. I'm going to call the police,' Bibi said, moving away from the cave entrance and removing her backpack to get her phone out.

But before she could make the call, a very weird person and a very large crab emerged from the smoke, coughing and rubbing their eyes. Bibi, who had been sitting down, stood up and stared open-mouthed.

'Are you okay?' she managed to splutter out on the crazy assumption that they spoke English, or even could speak at all.

But she had no need to worry, at least not about that particular language thing – although there were simply tons and tons of other things to be added to all of the others...

'Hello! I am Captain Jimmy Ocean,' the odd-looking boy replied while rubbing his eyes, 'and this is my very good friend, Bosun Jacob Crab. Jacob Crab is extraordinarily strong but very short of the sighted. I find it perfect beyond the sun's high altitude that you entered The Old Lookout Tower portal. Are the boots and collar a good size of fitting? Could I invite you to some Horrid Green Custard, we have a fresh brew which is more excellent than daydreams.'

The odd-looking boy, Captain Jimmy Ocean as he had announced himself, was made from plastic beach garbage in the same way the sailing boat was made. and he could speak, in an odd sort of way admittedly, but he could speak, which for plastic was fairly extraordinary and amazing.

Bibi sat down on her backpack and stared. She smiled weakly. It was all she could, in that very instance, think of doing.

The enormous crab, Bosun Jacob Crab as Captain Jimmy Ocean had introduced him, was carrying an old-fashioned, smoke-blackened kettle in his giant claw as he came clear of the smoke and into full view.

Bibi stared in disbelief at his size. No wonder, she thought, Old Tom's crab pots get '*smashed to smithereens*'. This is not possible, none of this is possible she was thinking, still holding her phone from when she was going to make the emergency call. And she did think of getting the giant crab photo to end all giant crab photos to send the dad – but he was holding a kettle! How could she send an image of a crab holding a kettle and be taken seriously?

Very carefully, and with great precision, Jacob Crab poured the steaming lime green liquid into three small scallop shells, which he had delicately balanced on a flat piece of rock.

'Best brew ever was,' he said to Bibi passing her a shell.

'Blow on it, though. 'Tis hot.'

Bibi audibly gasped, and spluttered, 'Thanks, I will,' and then lent down and whispered into Princess Liquorice's ear, 'Is it because I can understand you that I can now understand what crabs and plastic say, or has Playing Place Cove made me totally mad?'

Princess Liquorice growled, 'Is it time for a sausage roll? I'm starving.'

Bibi turned and faced Captain Jimmy Ocean who, still occasionally rubbing his eyes, was sitting on the grass gazing up at the sun. With her arms akimbo, using the firm tone that her mother used when correcting her school work when she had been slapdash, asked, 'How real is all of this? I was here the day before yesterday and Zawn Cove was normal. None of this was here: the cave was not here, the wooden jetty was not here, that very peculiar sailing boat now tied up to the jetty was not here, and most certainly there was not a giant crab here acting as a waiter. And there most absolutely definitely was not a person calling himself Captain Jimmy Ocean, who appears, not that I want to sound rude you understand, but appears to be made entirely of odd bits of plastic and stuff washed up on the beach. So, what is this all about? Messing up our beach with cave digging and polluting it with stinking green smoke is a serious business, you know.'

'What was real on Wednesday is not necessarily real on Saturday,' Jimmy Ocean replied enigmatically, while smiling broadly and lowering his gaze to the far horizon.

'Yes, I suppose...' Bibi started to say when the mass of green smoke cleared, revealing a hut built on a grassy platform to one side of the cave entrance. The hut was made entirely from old canvas and driftwood. 'And what's that?' Bibi cried in disbelief. '*Does it have planning permission?*' she asked, but immediately regretted saying it realising how like her mother she sounded.

'Everything is for a purpose, part of the grandest of grand projects,' Jimmy Ocean spoke dreamily, while continuing to gaze at the horizon.

'Are you looking for something?' Bibi asked, a bit annoyed that she was not being taken seriously and that this person had sort of just moved in and taken over 'her' beach without even saying 'would you mind?'

'A messenger,' Captain Jimmy Ocean replied. 'I am on the lookout for a messenger. But forgive me, there is gravity in lightness that perhaps goes unnoticed some years – have you spotted it?'

'I can't say that I have,' Bibi replied stroppily, and flew off down to the beach to have a serious think.

Princess Liquorice joined her while she skimmed pebbles across the water. 'I once read about *parallel worlds*.

I wonder if this is a *real* parallel world,' Bibi said, pensively. 'And that Captain Jimmy knew all about the boots and the collar and he called The Old Lookout Tower a portal.'

'And what's a portal? I might be a smart dog but why do you expect me to know everything?' Princess Liquorice moaned while scratching a hole in the sand.

'Quite simply, a portal is a gateway into another world,' Bibi said skimming a pebble, which bounced on the surface of the water eleven times before it plopped into a wave. 'And a parallel world – in case you might be interested – is like a step sideways from the world we are living in. I was going to say a step sideways from the *real world* but then I thought, who's to say if this world or the step sideways world, is the real world?'

'Is that what your mum writes about?' Princess Liquorice was already getting bored. She bored easily.

'No, Mum knows nothing about portals and step sideways parallel worlds and exciting stuff. She just does stuffy boring stuff – ocean plastic pollution and that.... Hey, wait,' Bibi paused thinking. 'He's made of tide-washed-up beach rubbish bits, the Captain Jimmy Ocean creation. Now that is a bit weird. Well it's all weird, of course, but that's kind of extra odd – the connection, I mean. Mum writing about it in the real world and now this Captain Jimmy Ocean thing in this sideways step-world that somehow we have become involved in.'

'Yes, it really is very odd, very curious. I wonder...' But she said no more, just continued searching for the perfect flat, not too heavy, not too light skimming stone to beat her eleven record.

'Was that Horrid Green Custard stuff good? I would have tried it, they didn't offer me any,' Princess Liquorice complained, dodging in and out of the breaking waves.

'Good? Good? It was totally foul. I only touched it with the tip of my tongue. Imagine rancid snot mixed with pickled rat's eye balls, hamster diarrhoea poo flavoured with cow pats, and you're a hundredth of the way to how totally disgusting it was. Uck, uck, uck!' Bibi put her fingers in her mouth and feigned retching.

'So, you hope it's not on the party food menu when we go to Lucy's birthday next week?' Princess Liquorice joked.

'Count me out if it is. Count me out if it's even in the cow shed being fed to the cows. Count me out if it's being fed to the pigs. Uck! Don't even talk about it. It was so gross.'

Princess Liquorice growled, 'Look, look, look at that lot.' Bibi glanced up from her stone skimming and was surprised that she was not totally surprised. It was as if she was settling in to this odd and very different world, as if what had only minutes ago been so abnormal was now the new normal. Was that scary or exciting, or both? She was not exactly sure.

'Crabs,' she said, 'more crabs, but this time normal, small, green-coloured crabs.' The crabs had climbed up the wooden jetty pilings and were scuttling along the jetty decking towards the beach. Jacob Crab was behind them, sort of shooing them forwards with the occasional swing of his giant claws.

'The Crab Gang from Zawn Cove,' he announced rather proudly, Bibi thought.

'Are they yours?' Bibi asked. 'Your family?'

'Some are,' he replied. Perhaps he smiled, perhaps he beamed with pride and pleasure, but there was no way of knowing because his carapace was ridged and he had absolutely no facial expression at all.

'They sing, they like to call themselves a band,' Jacob Crab said, putting his claw down so that they could climb on and then swinging his claw around so that Bibi could observe them closely.

'Hey, great idea. Can I get a selfie? The giant Jacob Crab together with the normal crab-size Crab Gang to show just how enormous he is. Perfect! Then I'll send it to my dad and cousins.'

'Whatever a selfie is, I'm the crab for it,' Jacob Crab said squeakily. He arched his claws upward in a macho pose, with Princess Liqcs hovering in the background making funny faces and sticking her tongue out.

Bibi excitedly took the shot, not for one second pausing to consider if it was at all possible. Which was, can you transmit images across parallel worlds or is there something like a technological block which prevents that happening?

She pressed send anyway.

It would either go or it would just get stuck, glued up somewhere in space/time, only to be discovered floating around by space archaeologists thousands of years in the future – when crabs, like dinosaurs, had died out. Bibi laughed to herself at the thought of future archaeologists trying to figure out just what exactly Jacob Crab was, because by then, according to her mum, the oceans would be dead, with all marine life having been killed off by eating rubbish plastic particles and the toxins that they attract.

It was about that moment that Bibi began to understand the full scale of this adventure. What had started out first thing in the morning in her bedroom as a bit of an odd tingle had, within the space of just over an hour, became awesomely immense.

Who would have thought that within such a short space of time she would have taken a selfie, together with a giant crab and a gang of singing crabs, sent it to Dad in Africa and the cousins in Spain, zoomed around with her own flying boots and touched with the very tip of her tongue the foulest tasting liquid in the universe and beyond – Horrid Green Custard?

On top of all of that, they had entered, Princess Liquorice and herself, a parallel world with a totally different set of doing-things rules. For instance, things were there that were not there before, like a jetty, like a cave, like a weird sailing boat, were suddenly there without any signs of building work or all of the normal messy things connected with new constructions and excavations.

Had Captain Jimmy sailed the *Ocean Flyer* to Zawn Cove alone? That was another question Bibi asked herself. Or, which seemed even more peculiar, had he somehow built it there on the beach? She had to admit that adjusting to doing-things-by-seemingly-magic rules took some getting used to.

'Ok, so what next?' she said to herself, looking around and seeing Jacob Crab carrying green barrels, one in each claw, across the beach and stacking them on a pile on the jetty. Captain Jimmy was rolling one down over the grass.

'Can I give you a hand?' Bibi called out.

'No, I have two and you will need both of yours for the voyage,' he called over his shoulder turning back to the cave to collect another barrel.

'What voyage?' Bibi shouted.

'To the Ocean Beyond, to The Big Whizzo. We sail a minute before the hour strikes,' he replied.

The barrel that Captain Jimmy had rolled down had stopped against a rock. Bibi rolled it around the rock and on down across the beach to the jetty. Jacob Crab picked it up and stacked it on the pile.

'What is that stuff?' Bibi asked Jacob Crab. 'It has a strange feel.'

'Horrid Green Custard with the flow ingredient extracted,' he replied.

'In the shape of a barrel?' Bibi questioned. 'In the shape of a barrel but without a barrel around it? Weird.'

'For rolling convenience, onboard *Ocean Flyer* it will be ballast convenience and when we arrive at The Big Whizzo it will magic Mermaid Stones and magic crystal sand convenience. It can be any convenience that you want and the taste is superb when it's liquid convenience,' and Jacob Crab smacked his feelery lips.

'Oh, I see,' puzzled Bibi, not understanding anything at all.

# - CHAPTER FOUR -

## AS FAR AS YESTERDAY AND BACK

'Captain Jimmy,' can you please stop for a moment and explain a few things. This voyage for instance, is it far? Voyages can be very dangerous you know, particularly long ocean voyages, and where is this Far Ocean anyway? I've never heard of it and I'm good at geography, it's one of my best subjects.'

'Where The Big Whizzo is,' he explained with an explanation which explained nothing.

'So, what is The Big Whizzo?' Bibi asked, brushing from her shorts a green, yellow and red fly, the like of which she had never seen before.

'A whirlpool in The Far Ocean, without better explanation. That's a fact that's as true as the fact that the moon is made from blue cheese,' Captain Jimmy had stopped rolling barrels and had flopped down on the grass, mopping his plastic brow with a torn piece of yellow neckerchief.

'How is it you can sweat?' Bibi asked, peering closer and inspecting his forehead.

'It's quite a phenomenon, you know. I only *look* like plastic,' he said.

'That's true, you do, really exactly like plastic. Plastic bottle tops, plastic spoons, a bit of mop handle I can see and numerous other bits brought in by the wind and the tide? And another thing, excuse me for being personal, but the way that you talk, it is very odd, you know. It's, well, it's as if some of the plastic cells of your brain have been put in a bit skew-whiff.'

Jimmy Ocean laughed, 'Thank you very much pleasantly. That's the very nicest wonder that anyone has ever said to me.'

Did Captain Jimmy actually blush? Bibi laughed and scrutinised his broken bits of multicoloured beach-bucket cheeks as close as she dared. She couldn't be sure.

'Okay, so what do you mean when you say that you only *look* like plastic when you clearly *are* made of plastic? Please explain that.' Bibi adjusted the peak of her cap to cut out the glare of the sun, scrunched up her eyes and fixed them on him.

'Do you know what an illusion is inside out?' he asked, pacing back and forth on the soft grass in a sort of scholarly way.

'Well, not exactly, but is that what you are, an inside-out illusion? Okay, I'll buy that. I suppose what you're trying to say is that you're a real person who's odd, made of plastic bits that create an illusion. That is a perfectly rationally stupid explanation that perfectly fits the circumstances that we are in – thank you for being so clear,' Bibi said, stroking Princess Liquorice's tummy. She was now lying beside her enjoying the warmth of the sun.

'One last question before we set sail, as we don't have a lot of time, as it must be just about one minute to the clock by now,' Bibi teased, as she replied in the same mad way that Captain Jimmy spoke.

'It is precisely by the hour. What was your question and you had better be in time for it?' Captain Jimmy had his hand to his eyes and was staring out to sea.

'My question is this. Why does the Horrid Green Custard have to be brewed here, in this newly created cave? Why go to all of the trouble of the cave, jetty and boat?'

'That is the best question this side of Wednesday,' Captain Jimmy replied, all the time staring harder and harder out to sea. 'Sulphur.'

'*Sulphur*?' Bibi repeated.

'Yellow sulphur mixed with blue fin potato fish brains rotted to stinking flavour and mashed with magic secrets and lots of stuff beyond the understanding of non-plastic

*Two Legs*.' Captain Jimmy's voice got louder and louder and the words *Two Legs* he shouted at the top of his very slightly plasticky voice.

'Am I a *Two Legs* then?' Bibi enquired 'Is that what you call me?'

'The doggie has four legs, the crabs have more legs, you have two legs and you are not of plastic construction – there is a logic in logic that is logical and that is the understanding of it.' Captain Jimmy stamped his foot as if he was a bit cross at having to waste time explaining what to him was logical and perfectly obvious, and by extension should be logical and perfectly obvious to every *Two Legs* on the planet.

Bibi was not so sure that being referred to as *Two Legs* was not a bit rude, but said nothing more about it. She had intended to ask about the flying boots and collar, plus lots of other mysteries, but felt that perhaps it was not quite the right moment. Captain Jimmy appeared to be getting more and more anxious as he paced back and forth, constantly staring way out to sea while sipping Horrid Green Custard from a shell.

Princess Liquorice woke from her snooze with a start. A naughty thought had awoken her, in a way that was perfectly normal; most of her thoughts were naughty, whether asleep or awake, but this was a particularly naughty, naughty thought. 'Perfect,' she thought to herself, the Crab Gang from Zawn Cove were lazing in a nearby rock pool. 'Just perfect!'

She took off, flew away from the rockpool and then, flying low, circled back heading towards the lounging, unsuspecting crabs from the direction of the sea.

A lot of the things that she had learned in her life were from Bibi, her owner. And because Bibi was a very smart girl for her age, Princess Liquorice was a very smart dog. But even though she was smart, the whole parallel world malarkey, not being something that she had heard talked about before, was an idea that she was finding difficult to understand, either fully, partly or even a little bit at all. And because Princess Liquorice had a thing about not understanding things, it had upset her snoozing so much that she was now feeling really grumpy.

Understanding things in the doggie world had a lot to do with sniffing and biting, and with Princess Liquorice the *proof* of anything was certainly in the biting.

So, biting was what she planned to do. Biting would give the definitive answer, pure and simple. Crunching a crab between her sharp terrier teeth would give her the proof that she was looking for – if the crabs crunched then they were real, and if they did not crunch then they were fantasy or a figment of a daydream or parallel-ish or whatever.

*But did she dare?*

She hovered, keeping low behind the seaweed-covered rock, glanced around and could see that Bibi, a little way off and higher up on the grassy slope, was still talking to Captain Jimmy, whose attention was on staring seaward. Rising up slightly, Princess Liquorice peered over the seaweed and into the pool. The entire Crab Gang was relaxing in a circle, holding claws.

*Did she dare?*

She edged closer, just half a metre, close enough to hear that they were humming a tune in harmony. Baring her teeth, she silently flew closer, centimetre by centimetre. The humming was getting louder and louder. At the moment she decided to pounce, there was a deafening *Clack! Clack!* sound right in her ear. Being totally focused on the rockpool, the Crab Gang and whether or not they would crunch, she had been totally unaware of anything creeping up behind.

Losing all flying control, she crashed down into the wet, slimy seaweed. On her back, she looked up and there above her was the terrifyingly enormous shape of Jacob Crab.

He reached out a claw. 'Sorry,' he squeaked, in his odd crabby squeaky voice helping her to her feet. 'Whenever I try quiet clacking it don't turn out right. Sorry if I scared you, like. Just trying to be a bit funny, nothing more,' he apologised, very delicately plucking bits of seaweed from her fur.

'Brilliant *clacking*,' Captain Jimmy called out. 'Oscar Shark heard the clack, which echoed to the day up there and beyond the horizon. Now he's heading this way with the *message*.' Captain Jimmy was excitedly running back and forth across the grass, yelling at the top of his plastic voice, 'The message, the message, the message, yeh!'

'Can you let me in on this?' Bibi shouted, grabbing hold of Captain Jimmy's arm to stop him running. 'What is this all-important blooming message?'

'From The Big Whizzo whirlpool mermaids, the message, the message.' Captain Jimmy wriggled free and ran higher up the bank to see further out to sea.

'I can see his fin, I can see his black dorsal fin slicing ocean waves,' Captain Jimmy cried, standing on tiptoes and pointing.

'Wow! He's fast!' Bibi gasped.

'As fast as a dream on a string with rockets.' Captain Jimmy's face was beaming with pleasure and excitement.

'And big! Wow! He's so big. Is he a great white?' Bibi was feeling the surge of excitement too. It was as if it was rushing forwards like a great shark-driven bow wave.

'Right Shark, he's a very rare Great Right Shark, named that way because right is right and that's what he is; right and rare, very ancient and most certainly, possibly the only Great Right Shark swimming the oceans from top to bottom in the present time - he's a Great Right Shark mystery.' Captain Jimmy jumped onto a rock, lifted his head, faced the wind shouting and then attempted a yodel which failed to get past the yo.

Oscar Shark roared into the jetty, and when the great tidal wave that his zooming in arrival had created receded down the beach, they all ran or scuttled down to meet him. Captain Jimmy sort of gave him a hug, although actually giving an enormous shark snouty mouth that rested on the end of the jetty a hug was almost really totally impossible.

Jacob Crab jumped onto his back and tweaked his fin in a friendly way.

'He has loads of teeth,' Bibi observed, not getting too close.

'Ask him if his teeth are getting bigger.' Captain Jimmy said to Jacob Crab. 'Because I, Jimmy Captain Ocean, gobbled up in confabulation, believe that they are, and looking very sharp too. Scary-zooper!'

'Scary-zooper,' Bibi laughed. 'Exactly right. Really scary-zooper, if you ask me.' Bibi edged a bit closer, peering at a deep scar that appeared to run right around his body just in front of his fin. 'And what's that?' she asked, pointing.

Jacob Crab had crabbed forwards so that he was resting

on Oscar Shark's head, just behind his sinister bulging black eyes.

'He says that he is worried about his teeth,' Jacob Crab reported. 'And he says other things are happening, worrying things, never-known-before things. He says he feels angry, and before he never knew what angry was. He says that The Far Ocean mermaids tell him it's the plastic as is the doing of it.'

'Does Jacob Crab speak for Oscar all of the time?' Bibi asked.

'Jacob Crab amplifies Oscar Shark's vocal vibrations through his shell,' Captain Jimmy said, making Bibi smile because it was the first sensible explanation that she had ever heard him make. And it made her wonder if perhaps he had been playing some sort of game with her previously.

'Has he never been able to speak to you, then?' Bibi was a bit curious because she could see that Jimmy and Oscar were friends and wondered how that happened if they were unable to communicate directly.

'Before he got tangled he could talk.'

'Tangled?' Bibi queried.

'Roped up,' Jimmy answered.

'Roped up?' Bibi queried again.

'Tangled in the fishermen's netting that cut into his shark body and left the great deep scar. The fear and the pain left him mute,' Captain Jimmy sighed, as if all was perfectly obvious and had no need of explanation.

'That's exactly what happens when the moon pulls a sock over its ear,' Bibi replied, grinning.

'Whatever is the meaning of that? That is a very peculiar way of talking,' Captain Jimmy gave Bibi a hard shake.

She laughed, and went 'boo' in his face. 'You have started to talk normally so I decided to talk how you used to talk,' she said and laughed and went 'boo' again.

'How sorry I am, and it was because upstairs got a lost way but is back in line now presently,' he said, keeping a very severe-looking face and then turning to Jacob Crab. 'The message, it is necessary to know all full details.'

Bibi touched the corner of his mouth with the tip of her finger. 'Smile,' she said teasingly. 'Smile, I know that you want to. If you want a funny talking competition then I can funny talk just as well as you can funny talk.'

'We must know the message with exact exactness,' he said to Jacob Crab, keeping a straight face despite Bibi continuing to tweak his mouth.

Jacob Crab scuttled over Oscar Shark's head onto the jetty and whispered into Captain Jimmy's ear.

'Then absolutely sure fire we will do that exactly so,' Captain Jimmy announced, swinging his arms around in a windmill fashion.

'What exactly are we to do?' quizzed Bibi with a frown, put out by the what she regarded as unnecessary whispering secrecy.

'Big Whizzo, voyage off to, and do it now very fast immediately,' Captain Jimmy ordered.

♬♪ 'Far over the ocean is a mermaid queen ♩ ♪
♪ All lost and hidden and not often seen ♪
♪ Horrid Green Custard is all she needs now ♪
♪ To complete the magic and make the vow ♪
♪ To clean the oceans of plastic and stuff ♪
♪ The Far Ocean is certainly dangerous and rough.' ♪

sang the Crab Gang from Zawn Cove.

'Princess Liquorice and I are coming,' Bibi said, cheerily waving her arms in windmill fashion as if that was some sort of start signal. 'And what about the all-important *message*?'

'Yes, the message, the message.' Captain Jimmy was dancing a little jig on the jetty while Jacob Crab loaded the 'barrels' of Horrid Green Custard, which immediately changed shape and weight when they were dropped into the *Ocean Flyer*, flowing beneath the floor boards and into the keel as ballast – the weight necessary to help keep the sailing boat from tipping over in the wind.

'The message, Jimmy,' Bibi repeated.

Oscar Shark coughed. Bibi glanced over her shoulder, putting her hand over her mouth and nose because his fishy breath was disgustingly foul. She took a step back. Were his teeth even bigger now, she asked herself a bit horrified? Something very odd was happening to the Great Right Shark who was still resting his chin on the end of the jetty and staring very strangely. Or at least it certainly looked like a strange stare to Bibi, but she had to admit that she had never looked a shark directly in the eye from what was no more than an arm's length or two or three... Well perhaps never... She was trying to remember. The teeth were certainly a big worry.

Princess Liquorice clearly thought them very scary too as she was not even on the jetty, but was back on the beach running in and out of the waves.

'Jimmy, look at those teeth. Is it my imagination or are they getting bigger by the minute?' Bibi asked, taking a few cautious steps back.

'The message, the message, I have it clearly in the boot of my memory. It is, it is... What did you ask me?' Captain Jimmy removed his blue-and-white spotted baseball cap and scratched his head.

'The message, Jimmy, the message,' Bibi reminded.

'Yes, exactly. I have it clearly to be spoken. At full moon

when the tide is at its totally maximum flooding height, The Big Whizzo whirlpool will be open and twisting downward full speed whizzing so that we can sail right down and in with the magic cargo of Horrid Green Custard for delivery to the mermaids of the Ocean Beyond... And moon and tide aligned and ready with The Big Whizzo will be in seven thousand one hundred and one seconds and counting down NOW,' Captain Jimmy shouted leaping aboard the *Ocean Flyer*, gripping the steering tiller and shouting, cast off and all aboard, all aboard and cast off.'

♪ 'Jimmy's scary alright ♪
♪ He even gives us a fright,' ♪
♪ 'A mermaid creation ♪
♪ Salty sea, a relation ♪
♪ But Jimmy's the boy for an ocean plastic fight,
that right.' ♪

sang the Crab Gang from Zawn Cove, as they madly scuttled aboard while Jacob Crab set sail with extraordinary speed, and for a giant crab, amazing dexterity.

# - CHAPTER FIVE -

## THE LOGBOOK THAT TURNS ITS OWN PAGES

The *Ocean Flyer* was fast. She skimmed over the waves as if powered by a magic wind. Bibi was sitting on the floor, sheltered by the raised deck from the flying spray.

Captain Jimmy was steering; legs braced, plastic hair flying, whistling a sea shanty. But the sound of the whistling was being taken by the wind, and it just looked as if his lips were pursed rather oddly.

'Captain Jimmy,' Bibi called out. 'How long to The Big Whizzo?'

He bent down and whispered in her ear, 'This mission is secret and time is not being counted.'

'What about the seven thousand odd seconds and counting down?' she asked, pretending to play his game.

'Discontinued, disconnected.' He stamped on the deck. 'And, by Jupiter, that's an order!'

'Cool! I'll text Mum and say that I'll be back last year

sometime, but not to worry about my Christmas present just yet,' Bibi laughed taking her phone from her backpack.

The message, the little fib, which she actually sent said:

*Sleeping over at Lucy's, I'll call later. Not to worry. Love you. Xxx*

'Well, Liqcs, that should buy us a moment or two, or a day taken from last week – Lucy's cottage in Sleepy Hollow had no mobile signal and the landline hadn't worked for weeks. So, let's see what The Big Whizzo is all about. What about a sausage roll and a sticky bun?'

'*Not to worry*,' she had said in the text to Mum. Well, Bibi smiled to herself, what was there to worry about? She had sandwiches, sausage rolls, sticky buns and a bottle of water. They had magic flying boots and a flying collar. They were sailing away to an unknown destination called The Big Whizzo whirlpool located in somewhere called The Far Ocean, in a very weird, magically fast sailing boat with a boy made out of bits of plastic who could talk, an enormous crab, a gang of green crabs that sang, led by a Great Right Shark with teeth getting bigger all of the time for some mysterious reason – *so what was there to worry about?*

Bibi's smartphone rang. 'No, Mum, I won't forget to collect the lettuces and tomatoes from Mary Richards. Not at Lucy's yet. Love you. Bye.'

Jacob Crab was on the floorboards next to Bibi, sharing a very small part of his sticky bun with the Crab Gang from Zawn Cove. 'That scar on Oscar Shark,' she asked him, 'Captain Jimmy said he got tangled in a rope. How did he get free?'

♬♪'Sticky bun, yummy, yum, yum ♪
♪ Into your tummy and out of your bum,' ♬♪

cut in the Crab Gang from Zawn Cove.

'Captain Jimmy Ocean saved him, he did. Cut the rope. That's how they got to be mates. He's loyal as ever a shark can be loyal, if you get my meaning,' Jacob Crab said, sucking some sticky icing from the end of his great claw.

'You mean he might not always be a loyal mate?' Bibi asked, still not able to get the thought of the lines of strangely enlarging teeth in Oscar Shark's mouth out of her mind.

'Your words, not mine, wink, wink,' said Jacob Crab.

'And where is he now, this *'psychologically disturbed'* and, if you ask me, rather oversized, Great Right Shark with scary teeth and a scary look in his eye?' Bibi asked Jacob Crab.

'He's a-guiding us, he's a-guiding us to The Big

Whizzo,' Jacob Crab explained, bending one of his claws back over his carapace and pointing ahead. 'Swims like a shark torpedo, he does.'

Captain Jimmy handed the steering over to Jacob Crab, sat down beside Bibi and opened a small hatch door in the floor. It was not something that Bibi had noticed before, and the thought flashed through her mind that it was very possible that things appeared only when Captain Jimmy wanted them to, and that certainly allowed for many possibilities – the Zawn Cove cave, jetty, flying boots and collar among them.

From the smallish space beneath the hatch, Captain Jimmy took out a thickish book and handed it rather solemnly to Bibi.

'This is the ship's logbook,' he said. The rather exotic ship's logbook had a gold front cover and a sparkly purple back cover.

'Thank you, very lovely,' she replied, taking it. And just when she went to open the gold front cover, it opened itself. 'Well, that's sort of a rather novel feature,' she grinned, as she closed the cover and watched it open again. This time, two more pages turned before stopping on a page that read:

*Start log entries here, name, official crew position, ship's time, ship's position East of Greenwich... and write neatly.*

'It's rather a bossy ship's logbook,' Bibi laughed, testing the opening and closing and page flicking a few more times. She even turned it back to front and upside down, but each time it returned to the 'Start log entries here' page.

Then, from out of his shorts' pocket, Captain Jimmy produced a bendy green pen. The ballpoint pen had an orange cork on top.

'What's the cork for?' Bibi asked, bending the pen back and forth and finally tying it in a knot.

'Well, so that it floats in the case of shipwreck,' Captain Jimmy replied nonchalantly, as if it was completely obvious and that a shipwreck was some sort of everyday occurrence.

'And what if we all sink and only the pen floats? What good will that be?' Bibi questioned. But before Captain Jimmy could reply with some of his daft logic, she changed the subject. 'Ok, so now that I have a ship's logbook and a bendy funny-feeling pen, what do you want me to write?'

'The pen will write, just touch it to the page,' Captain Jimmy said, smiling his neo-plastic smile, which Bibi read to mean *this is just another funny and mysterious day.*

Bibi did as instructed. The pen wrote in green 'Bibi Lopez-Miller'.

'Love this!' Bibi exclaimed. 'Can I keep it? Just perfect for doing school work.'

'We are in a vital speeding rush,' Captain Jimmy

insisted. 'Please to continue, pertinently important to diurnally update. That is, to write in it daily and at least every hour, or certainly by the minute.'

The pen then wrote beside 'official crew position' First Mate Bibi Lopez-Miller SAF'.

'This is amazing. By the way, what does SAF stand for?' Bibi asked, while allowing the pen to fill in the time and ship's current latitude and longitude positions.

'SAF – *Skilled At Flying*,' Captain Jimmy sighed. 'It's the pen being funny. It might have to be reset if it fails to behave professionally. Please untie the knot in the pen – it could be that it is displeasured and that the unprofessional joking is Horrid Green Custard protest expression.'

Bibi straightened the pen out. 'You mean, this is Horrid Green Custard too?' She was suddenly not so sure that she liked it.

'Horrid Green Custard in flexi-gel form with thinking ingredient added. It's the thinking ingredient level that might need adjusting back in the lab.'

'The lab, the laboratory, and where's that? Is that in the Zawn Cove cave too?' Bibi asked while bending the pen into a U shape to tease its brain into writing something else 'unprofessional'.

'Down beneath the Ocean Beyond, down The Big Whizzo whirlpool,' Captain Jimmy hissed in her ear.

'That's where it is. All secrets to be kept under beneath hat without uttering a sound.'

'Aye, aye, Captain,' Bibi saluted. She was not exactly sure why she saluted, but perhaps it was because Captain Jimmy had such an authoritative way of hissing.

'This is a vital record of our vital voyage on this very vital mission that is vital, and all of the very vital information about this vital voyage has to be constantly updated vitally,' Captain Jimmy pronounced.

'Yes, Sir.' Bibi saluted again. It was getting to be real fun. 'All vital info to be entered into the ship's logbook '*by the hour and certainly every minute*'.

'That is as correct as without a doubt,' Captain Jimmy said, standing and saluting as he spun in a circle before returning to face Bibi. 'You will please do me the kindness of making the following gold cover entry':

'This is the most vital voyage in all of the long history of voyages of adventure and discovery. This voyage is to save the oceans from being killed. If this voyage fails then Wednesday is cancelled forever,' Jimmy said. But when Bibi read what the pen wrote she almost burst into tears.

*All that Captain Jimmy says is true, but what he also wanted to say, and was unable to because emotion has not yet been installed in him, was this. Something terrible is happening to my friends, to Oscar Shark, to Jacob Crab. We laugh about them getting bigger and bigger and sometimes angry, and teeth getting bigger and sharper, but the beautiful oceans are now poisoning them. And none of us really knows what to do – sea birds being choked, turtles and sharks tangled and strangled by plastic ropes and every marine creature poisoned. How can this happen? Who would be so stupid as to poison all of this amazing wonder and beauty? Maybe the Horrid Green Custard will be the solution, the magic Mermaid Stones, but maybe not. Prof Gilbert Octopus, working for mermaids from the Ocean Beyond, made me out of plastic so that I could go out into the human people world to get help, but instead of helping they just every day make the oceans more and more polluted with millions and millions of more pieces of toxic plastic. I've been made to be a bit jokey, but in my plastic heart I'm not jokey. I'm just crying but without being able to cry.*

Bibi gave Captain Jimmy a great big hug. 'Jolly lucky that I brought sandwiches,' she said, wiping her eyes. 'Seems like it's going to be a long voyage... With lots of important stuff to do.'

Captain Jimmy shrugged Bibi off. 'Yes, well, that's it, got to get going...' Logbook entry continues:

*12 noon, Whatsupday, 11th Juneberry, steering South, South West, destination Ocean Beyond, The Big Whizzo, deep in the whirling plastic wastes of the Oceans circulatory circulation currents central most massive vortex.*

This time, the flexi Horrid Green Custard pen wrote what it was told to write. Bibi, wondering if it had run out of its AI (Artificial Intelligence) quota, tied it in a knot again and let it write.

It wrote '*Snotnose*'.

'I love you!' she cried. 'Captain Jimmy, can I keep the pen? I love it, I just love it.'

'It's yours. We'll get more from The Big Whizzo.'

Bibi untied it, straightened it, gave it a little kiss and slipped it into a zipped-up compartment in her backpack.

The logbook had waxed pages, to prevent them getting soggy when wet Bibi presumed. A rather cool touch she thought to herself as she made lots of notes; some coded, some minutely written and some for all crabs and captains made of plasticky bits to read.

Using her special magnifying glass, she observed the page-turning process very closely, but was unable to see any turning mechanism. Very cool indeed, she muttered to herself. Very, very cool.

At home, Bibi kept a diary that she wrote in in her own special code; sort of 'Spanglish' with symbols. Writing notes (secret notes, adventure notes, notes about dreams – even nightmares) was one of her favourite things to do, so she got straight to work in the ship's logbook.

Also, hunkering down out of the wind and spray and focusing on writing kept her mind from wandering to thoughts of Oscar Shark, his massive size, his enlarging teeth and the very strange look in his eyes of which she kept getting flash backs.

From gold front to back she wrote *OFFICIAL BUSINESS* but from the logbook's purple back cover going forwards she used her secret code to write about flying boots, singing crabs, the prospect of Ocean Beyond mermaids and all of the weird stuff that had happened ever since entering the Old Chapel Lookout Tower.

All of the writing in her purple section of the ship's logbook she wrote using her own pen – could the flexi Horrid Green Custard pen be trusted? She smiled at the thought of having it and how she could use it at home. Could it be trained, she wondered. Wow! That was something to think about. And would it be able to understand her code? That was something to be very careful about.

Bibi was just wondering if she could go as fast with her boots on full power as the *Ocean Flyer* could sail when

Captain Jimmy shouted, 'Is Oscar Shark still in sight, Bosun Jacob Crab?'

'It's no good asking a crab that. They're as short-sighted as ducks with their heads in mud,' said First Mate Bibi Lopez- Miller. 'I'll take a look.'

Fighting her way forwards against the wind and spray, Bibi clambered up onto the foredeck, held tightly to the mast, steadied herself and peered out across the sparkling sunlit ocean and white foamy waves.

'No, nothing!' she shouted, scanning the waves ahead, and then pausing for the *Ocean Flyer* to rise up on a crest before searching again. 'Can't see that Great Right Shark friend of yours anywhere; are you sure he's reliable?'

Turning to get down, she glanced up at Captain Jimmy on the steering tiller.

'Oh no! Jimmy! Behind you. Down! Duck! Get down!' she screamed as she flung herself down onto the floorboards, grabbed Princess Liquorice and rolled beneath the shelter of the foredeck where the Crab Gang from Zawn Cove were rehearsing.

All Bibi could see were teeth – rows and rows of white glistening teeth. Teeth, and an enormous, yawning wide-open shark's mouth roaring up behind the *Ocean Flyer*, gigantic enough to devour ship and crew in one great chomping bite.

But instead of snapping his mouth shut, he roared past, tossing the *Ocean Flyer* up on an enormous wave. In a second, he was gone, far ahead, a dark shape on the distant horizon.

Captain Jimmy had been thrown over the side by the sudden lurch. Bibi saw him go, grabbed a rope to hold on to, leant over the side and got hold of his hand.

'Hold on, hold on, Jimmy! Jacob Crab, grab him before he gets swept away!' Bibi yelled, feeling that Captain Jimmy was slipping from her grip. But Jacob Crab had been thrown onto his back and was struggling to right himself.

At that moment, Princess Liquorice did an amazing thing. Taking a rope end in her mouth, she took off and flew round and round in tight circles until the rope was tightly knotted around Captain Jimmy's outstretched hand. And then, with her collar on max power, she lifted him right out of the water and plopped him back into the boat.

'Can't have any more rubbishy plastic in the ocean,' she barked, and gave herself a massive shake.

'That doggie is now the ship's official mascot-y thingy, to be entered in the logbook,' Jimmy Ocean spluttered.

'Mascot-y thingy, what's that? Can *mascot-y* be eaten, and if not I'm sticking with sausage rolls,' Princess Liquorice growled, feeling sort of miffed.

'He's grown very large,' Bibi said, nodding her head

towards the front, almost a bit scared to say his name out loud. 'I mean enormous. And did you see the look in his eye? Very mean looking.'

'It's the speed – he's taking in plastic particles by the tonne, 'e is. Mouth open wide and all that furious swimming. Thinks that he's filling up on plankton and the like but it's just plastic, all ruddy plastic bits, an' toxic an' all,' gasped Jacob Crab, finally flipping himself back over.

'I don't trust him, Captain Jimmy,' Bibi said firmly. 'I never liked the look in his eye back at Zawn Cove and now I think that he's turned nasty, really nasty... Gone rogue.'

'Mutated, like,' chipped in Jacob Crab.

'He brought the message,' Captain Jimmy said, but not sounding as if he was very sure about anything himself. 'He was my friend. He brought the message,' he repeated.

'But what if it was not the right message?' Bibi asked. 'Not the right instructions, not the right directions? What if he is leading us into a trap?'

'But why ever?' Captain Jimmy was chewing his plastic finger and leaving bite marks in it.

'Don't do that.' Bibi pulled his hand from his mouth. 'It's gross.'

♬♪ 'Lots of people like plastic ♪
♪ To some it's just totally fantastic ♬♪'

♪ Sheikhs that sell oil – they like it ♬♪'
♬♪ Orientals that make toys – they love it ♪
♪ Money people that make money – simply adore it ♪
♪ Perhaps it's only a few that deplore it,' ♬♪'

lamented the Crab Gang from Zawn Cove.

'That is very true,' Bibi said, clapping. 'So, what if Oscar Shark has become a monster? What if Oscar Shark Monster has been bought? What if Oscar Shark Monster is working for the enemy: the plastic makers, the plastic users, the millions and millions of single plastic bag carriers that care nothing about clean oceans and healthy sea creatures and all of that '*nonsense*,' as they would see it? What if Oscar Shark Monster is now and agent of *The Stupids*?'

# - CHAPTER SIX -

## STEROID-ICLES OR WHAT?

'Old Tom...' Bibi started to say before Jacob Crab exploded in anger, spitting out bits of the hummus and cucumber sandwich that Bibi had just handed out.

'Don't use filthy words like that. 'I'll SMASH THAT OLD TOM'S CRAB POTS TO SMITHEREENS WHEN WE RETURNS TO THE COVE, YOU SEE IF I DON'T! DAMN HIM FOR CRAB CATCHING!' Jacob Crab helped himself to a claw-full of hummus and cucumber sandwiches, and lumbered off to join the Crab Gang from Zawn Cove beneath the foredeck, muttering crossly to himself about Old Tom's crab catching activities.

'Sorry, Jacob Crab,' Bibi called out. 'Didn't mean to upset you, but I was just reminded what my friend in Playing Place Cove said the last time I saw him: 'T*hey'ms on steroid-icles*,' he said. Meaning the crabs that he was catching were getting bigger and bigger.' That part she whispered in Captain Jimmy's ear. 'What if The Stupids have let it be known to certain sea creatures that eating plastic is some brilliant fast seafood? Perhaps even added something extra poisonous or steroid-icle bulking-up ingredient? And Oscar Shark Monster has fallen for the trick, or scam, or cynical manipulation of the entire marine world so that they can sell more plastic by persuading humans that bigger fish means more tonnage to catch and more profits? Are The Stupids that evil?'

Captain Jimmy, scratching his head, found a small piece of seaweed. 'Look!' he cried, holding the tiny green piece out for Bibi to examine.

'It's very small. Are you sure it's seaweed? I'll take a look with my very special magnifying glass. Don't mention that to Jacob Crab,' she whispered, 'because Old Tom gave it to me.'

Carefully, Bibi examined the sliver of seaweed. 'It has specks on it, multicoloured specks,' she announced.

'Plastic,' said Captain Jimmy spitting the word out. 'That's horrid, but the important thing is the seaweed. The seaweed means that we are approaching the Sargasso Clingweed Rotation.'

'And that's the right direction?' Bibi asked, feeling more excited than worried.

'Yes, yes.' Captain Jimmy was standing turning this way

and that sniffing here and sniffing there.

'Can you sniff it? Is it sniff-able? Is this Sargasso Clingweed Rotation a sniff-able place?' Bibi was sniffing too but could only smell salty air.

'Among us seafaring folk, the Sargasso Clingweed Rotation is a place of mystery, suspicion and DREAD. There are ancient tales of pirate ships, like *Black Raven*, my old ship, drifting in circles for all time, trapped in the fearful clinging weed that is gathered by the swirl of the ocean currents and now there is plastic mixed in – billions, trillions of pieces. Clingweed sucks poison from the plastic and the toxic stink drifts in the dead air,' Captain Jimmy intoned, 'and that is what I am sniffing for: the morbid stink of lifeless ocean and the rotting hulk of the Raven and the bleached skeletons of my cut-throat crew.'

'Jimmy,' Bibi gave him a shake. 'Are you okay?'

His eyes flipped back into focus, 'Is it time for a sip of hot Horrid Green Custard before lights out, then?' he said, shaking his head and squinting at the bright sunlight as if he had just woken.

Bibi waved her hand back and forth in front of his eyes to get his focus sorted out, because he appeared totally disorientated. 'I bet I know what's happened,' Bibi laughed, giving Captain Jimmy another friendly shake. 'All this weird talk of drifting pirate ships. I think that your creator, whoever that was, played a bit of a joke and slipped a few random old-timer sea-dog brain cells into your head, and when they randomly connect, then... wow... you go old-timer, pirate-captain loopy. Wish I had some brain cells like that. Imagine... What about ancient Greek brain cells, or Genghis Khan brain cells (just a sprinkling, because he was mostly nasty)? Jimmy, stop sniffing, why are you still sniffing? It's just the dodgy brain cells. What about sharing a sticky bun? Or, try inhaling Horrid Green Custard fumes from the bilge. That could clear your head, particularly the HGC fumes.'

'Got it, by whizzy, whizzo and down The Big Whizzo. I've got the focal point of the location directionally located. That way!' he shouted, ran to the side of the *Ocean Flyer*, tripped and fell in.

Luckily, he still had the rope attached to his hand that Princess Liquorice had wound around before, so Jacob Crab was able to haul him back aboard without fuss. But as he did so, Captain Jimmy was still pointing as if his finger was a magnetic needle, and, whichever way you turned it, it flicked back to its original direction.

♬♪ 'Captain Jimmy can sniff it there is no doubt ♬
♬♪ Of course he can he has a plastic snout ♪
Was he ever a pirate? We're not so sure ♬♪
♬♪ But lots of odd things happened in days of yore

♬ The thing is now he has the sniff ♪
♪ Not that anyone else can smell the whiff,' ♬♪

sang the Crab Gang from Zawn Cove.

Bib was sitting on the floor with the ship's logbook in her lap open to the purple section – her personal section. 'One thing that I have on my list of questions to ask is: are we zipping over the waves in a bubble of magic, a mist of illusion, or are we in a parallel world and our real-life world is just over there somewhere? Even within reaching distance or throwing-a-ball distance or, a bit disgustingly, spitting distance?'

And just out of curiosity, how do you build all of the stuff, and so quickly? My dad took two weeks to put a flat-pack shed together and that only needed a few screws. It's like you just have to flick your fingers. Is that right?'

'All built in the Nick of Time,' Jimmy Ocean replied, standing up to his full height of 888 millimetres and smiling broadly. 'All was built in The Nick of Time.'

'So, when was this Nick of Time exactly. Was it the Nick of Time yesterday?'

'Well, it was the Nick of Time... as of course the Nick of Time is,' Jimmy Ocean replied a bit dismissively, clearly immediately losing interest in the subject.

'The Big Whizzo. Was that built in the Nick of Time

too, or has it always been there? Is it real, a real whirlpool? Is it a thought, a dream... a nightmare, even? Are we going to end up like that pirate ship of yours from before that you imagined, what was it you said, *Black Raven*? Are we going to end up drifting around, rotting with all of the other stuff in the Sargasso Clingweed Rotation for ever and ever in some space without time or place?'

Bibi felt her backpack that was resting against her leg twitch alarmingly. She opened it. The zipped-up compartment where she had put the flexi HGC pen was hopping up and down. As soon as she opened it the pen leapt into her hand and nestled between her fingers with its tip twitching.

'Ok, let's see what you want to write,' she said, turning the ship's logbook around and opening the official gold section and holding the pen against a blank page.

*It's terrible being in there. I have never been so badly treated in all of my days of being a ballpoint. It is quite intolerably dark. I get tossed around without any care for my fine tip and there is nothing at all to write on...*

Bibi read it and laughed. 'Well, now that you've got that out of your system do you have anything illuminating to write?'

*Twaddle Bonce, snot nose!*

'Choice! What you need is a name. Liqcs, what shall I call the pen?' Princess Liquorice opened just one eye, indicating that her level of interest in pen naming was not really very high.

'I know,' Bibi had an idea. 'What about SnotTip? How do you like the sound of that, SnotTip?'

♫ 'SnotTip, SnotTip soon to end up
in the rubbish tip,' ♪

the Crab Gang from Zawn Cove started up, but then stopped and shuffled off when Bibi put her finger to her lips for fear that their song might upset the touchy SnotTip even more.

Because, it was just possible that SnotTip knew secrets. Secrets that Bibi was very keen to find out and secrets that Captain Jimmy was not very readily revealing.

As a test, Bibi used the HGC green flexi SnotTip to write Has Captain Jimmy Ocean ever been a pirate?'

But instead of writing that, SnotTip wrote

*Never look over your shoulder without thinking about the next step first.*

# - CHAPTER SEVEN -

## JELLY BEANS AND THINGS

Bibi went forwards to where Jacob Crab was crouched beneath the foredeck. 'Jacob Crab, I am here to apologise for being a dirty, human, plastic, polluting creature. For ever going in Old Tom's boat, for talking about crab pots, for not particularly liking Horrid Green Custard and for anything else that you can think of that I've done to upset you. Would you like a jelly bean from the jar of 'specials' in Granny Bluebell's shop?'

Jacob Crab gave Bibi Lopez-Miller a very gentle crab hug and then very delicately took one green jelly bean from the white paper bag that Bibi was offering. 'I would just like to ask you a simple question. How do my boots and Princess Liquorice's collar work?'

'Easy as lounging in a rockpool. Anti-matter-particles-that-fall-upwards-gravity-control-negative-mass-positive-mass-repelling,' Jacob Crab gabbled, a little flustered after getting a bit carried away with 'the hug'.

'*Well*, that's simple enough,' gasped Bibi, and was totally flabbergasted that SnotTip wrote it down in very clear long hand but at super short-hand speed.

'Cool answer,' chipped in Princess Liquorice. 'Like your style, big boy.'

'Those green jelly beans are right delicious,' Jacob Crab said, glancing greedily at the open bag.

'Please, here, have them. I have more in my backpack. Share them with the Crab Gang from Zawn Cove.

'Well, as you explained that so *simply* and SnotTip wrote it down very efficiently, could you explain one other thing that both Princess Liquorice and I have found confusing? *Invisibility*. We noticed, when we were back at Zawn Cove, where in fact we first put the magic flying boots and the magic flying collar, that they appeared to... well, not just appeared to, they definitely did... make us totally invisible to human people...'

'And also,' barked in Princess Liquorice, 'that Dalmatian that was with them didn't give a sniff for me, which I find disrespectful or even rude. Dogs always sniff dogs' bottoms. It's the rule and what dog politeness is all about.'

'All to do with *parallel-ikity space*,' Jacob Crab replied, gingerly nipping at the hard outside of an orange jelly bean shell.

'*Parallel-ikity space,*' Bibi repeated. Was her brain turning to a sort of mush, she wondered? In fact, she did touch the top of her head in case it was getting squidgy but it seemed okay. 'Well, thank you.'

Jacob Crab scuttled off and shared the beans with the Crab Gang from Zawn Cove, who immediately starting fighting to get inside of the bag.

*Parallel-ikity space is like being an invisible shadow. The big crab dumbo should have explained that, SnotTip had written. All brawn and no brain. What is the world on the edge of the world coming to?*

Bibi tied SnotTip into a fairly tight knot and put him, her, it into the pocket of her shorts and quickly buttoned down the flap before there were anymore flexi HGC ballpoint escape attempts or snotty remarks written in the official ship's logbook.

'Captain Jimmy, what are you doing now?' Bibi gasped, looking up from her own purple logbook jottings. 'You've already fallen into the sea twice in the *last week of moments* and the third time might not be so lucky. And anyway, there's no one steering. Isn't that dangerous?'

'She's on auto straight-sailing pilot, newly installed,' he shouted down from the masthead.

'Is that another just-in-time-gismo?' Bibi shouted back, laughing. 'Come on down before you fall. Are you still looking for the Sargasso Clingweed Rotation? If you are, you're more likely to find it by looking through the *correct* end of the telescope.'

She could feel SnotTip twitching in her shorts pocket and, knowing that him, her or it was crazy to escape, gave her pocket a light tap. 'Remember who's boss, SnotTip,' she hissed in, having lifted the flap slightly.

Captain Jimmy turned the telescope around the right way, let out a piercing yell and crashed down from the top of the mast, bounced over the rigging ropes, slid down the belly of the great mainsail and, with a bang and a wallop, onto the floorboards, which smashed so that he ended up to his neck in Horrid Green Custard jelly.

With loads and loads of dripping HGC clinging to his hand and arm, his nose and hair, he pointed and, in a very weak voice, said, 'An *island*.'

♪ 'There is no *island* here, where only sea should be ♫
♪ Flipping heck, could there really be –
does it have a palm tree?
♫ This is an ocean that's empty – apart from
weed and junk ♪
♪ If there is an island here then, dear me,

we're all sunk ♬
♬ Unless, oh no, it really can't be true ♬
♬ Is he back, is he bigger, is he more gruesome too?' ♪

lamented the Crab Gang from Zawn Cove, taking shelter in the folds of a spare piece of sail.

# - CHAPTER EIGHT -

## CHOCOLATE BROWNIE TO THE RESCUE

Captain Jimmy was strangely subdued. Bibi pulled him up out of the Horrid Green Custard jelly with a big slurpy sucking sound, and flicked globules of it off him until at least his eyes and ears were mostly cleaned out.

'It's an island,' he repeated, 'an island. Heave-to the sails, to a stationary stop, Jacob Crab,' he ordered, in a voice which, for Captain Jimmy, was very quiet and disturbingly distant. Bibi wondered if perhaps he was suffering from shock after his fall or had a concussion, even.

'Don't be daft,' she said to herself. 'Plastic doesn't get concussed... But then, on the other hand, Captain Jimmy clearly does have a very odd set of brain cells which could have been badly shaken up – but was it the fall, or was it...? Liqcs, with me. We are going flying.'

At first, Bibi could not believe what she was seeing. The ocean ahead was not deep blue but multicoloured. There were no waves even though the wind was blowing – it was as if someone had placed an enormous, really, really, miles and tens or hundreds of miles wide carpet over the whole ocean before them.

Bibi flew down and grabbed her binoculars from her backpack. SnotTip was wriggling in her shorts pocket, clearly not being used to flying, but she ignored the HGC ballpoint and zoomed back up to where Princess Liquorice was loop-the-looping.

'It's plastic,' Bibi said in astonishment. 'Trillions and trillions of pieces of plastic. Plastic and weed matted together. Buoys and bottles, crates and cups and old toys. Everything, just everything. Just the most terrible rubbish tip all here, all floating here.'

Bibi zipped back down to the deck to report. 'It's a garbage patch as far as the eye can see. Just an ocean of floating plastic rubbish tightly packed together. And impenetrable for any sailing craft, if you want my opinion.'

'The Sargasso Clingweed Rotation. Did you spot the *Black Raven*? Is she still drifting in forever circles? And the island, what about the island? The island where there is no island, where no island should be,' Captain Jimmy sighed, still appearing completely dizzy and disorientated.

'I'll go higher and take a look for the island. Just take it easy, Jimmy. But tell me, is this the way to The Big Whizzo whirlpool, and are we in the right place?'

'In olden times, it was just the Clingweed, *in them real good Black Raven pirating days,*' Captain Jimmy sort of started to reminisce but only briefly. 'But with the ocean currents rotating round and sweeping and blowing and drifting and bringing in all of the thrown-away plastic, it's clung to the Clingweed.' Captain Jimmy himself appeared to be drifting a bit, too, and Bibi was seriously considering giving him a shake to see if it would get his probably Lego-like brain cells to slot back together.

'Of course,' she thought. 'If he had an on/off switch, that, perhaps, that would be the answer. After all, it always did the trick whenever her laptop want screwy.'

While pretending to flick off the last bits of HGC jelly, she sneakily looked around, but could see nothing that was obviously a switch.

'Ok, so we're on the edge of the Sargasso Clingweed Rotation... *and apart from your pirating exploits long ago*, which we are trying to forget,' she said in a very low voice, 'presumably you've been here before, because you tell me that you were made by the Ocean Beyond mermaids, and the Ocean Beyond mermaids live down in The Big Whizzo whirlpool. So, two questions. One, was the plastic pollution as bad as it is now or is it a seasonal thing? And two, which direction is The Big Whizzo, exactly?'

Captain Jimmy pointed. 'In the direction of the very thickest part of the Sargasso Clingweed Rotation.'

'Well, that's just great! It's impossible to get through, Jimmy, just impossible. And even if we penetrated a bit, it's vast, just vast,' Bibi said, feeling really disappointed that she was going to miss out on what she imagined would be the super waterslide part of whizzing down The Big Whizzo. 'Well, never mind then. I am getting a bit short of sticky buns, though.'

'It's in the centre,' Captain Jimmy said. 'The centrifugal vortex of screaming terror.'

'In the centre,' Bibi repeated, shaking her head. 'Well, I suppose that it had to be. Where else?'

'It's vital,' Captain Jimmy said with a big intake of breath.

'Vital to get through, vital to deliver the Horrid Green Custard that you've squelched all over the place? It might be vital to saving the oceans from more of this mess, but it's like pictures that I've seen of pack ice but this is pack plastic – to get through pack ice you need an ice breaker, and to get through this you'd need a powerful plastic breaker, which we don't have.'

'What about the island?' Captain Jimmy asked.

'Oh, yes, the island. I'd forgotten about that. But what does it matter? In any case we have to turn back, don't we?'

Captain Jimmy smiled and rotated his head as if he was easing a stiff neck. 'Would you please fly up aloft towards upwards and observe the directional bearings of the island?'

'Well, you are sounding very much better – I had difficulty making sense of any of that, except, the island. Ok, I'll check it out. And just you get those words really tangled up, and I'll know that you've made a full recovery,' Bibi joked and flew up with her binoculars around her neck, SnotTip still niggling away in her pocket.

From higher up than before, Bibi surveyed the scene of vile pollution. As far as the distant horizon, which was miles and miles away, perhaps as much as 30 or even 50, it was the same. Nothing but tightly packed plastic.

But then she saw something different, and, studying the area closely through her binoculars, she saw that there was a fairly large patch of open water, of relatively plastic-free water. And as she studied it even more carefully she saw that it was moving. It was rotating very slowly on its outer edge, but towards the centre it looked as if the rotation was faster.

'That's it,' she said to herself. Yes, that's it. It must be. It must be the outer edge of The Big Whizzo.'

But then, something else caught her attention, something large and moving towards the *Ocean Flyer*. Out in the open ocean, among the plastic, but among the more loosely packed plastic on the edge of the plastic garbage patch. Adjusting the focusing screw she zoomed in... It was the island and it was *moving*.

It was not an island with palm trees, a coral reef and a sparkling lagoon. It was a browny-grey coloured hump, which had large fins, angry bulging black eyes, an enormous open mouth and more teeth than Granny Bluebell had boiled sweets in her many shelves of glass jars in her Playing Place Cove shop.

Not only that, if that was not bad enough, it appeared to have tentacles, really ginormous tentacles. And the deformed tentacles had grown out of the hideous scar which went right around his body and looked raw and red where his body had grown and grown and had hideously expanded. It was the most grotesque and horrible creature that Bibi had ever seen, and she shivered and went cold all over at the realisation of what the toxic plastic had done to Oscar Shark Monster.

When Bibi recovered from the shock of what she had seen in her binoculars, she shouted, 'Captain Jimmy! It's Oscar Shark Monster and he's enormous! And he's terribly mean looking and he's heading this way with his enormous mouth open and at very high speed... And his teeth.... He's got masses and they've grown... Wow, they're horrible and they look dangerously sharp... We need to get out of here and FAST!' Bibi was shouting as she zoomed back down with Princess Liquorice barrel-rolling in and doing a perfect four-paw landing on the after deck.

Captain Jimmy was calmly tying a piece of thin rope around a yoghurt pot that he had retrieved from the sea.

'We don't have time for craftwork, Jimmy. He's less than half a mile away. He's heading straight for us and you can tell by his cruel eyes... Oh my dog... He's going to gobble us. He's so enormous now. We need to escape, we need full speed and more... Jimmy, are you listening?' Bibi banged her feet hard on the floorboards. 'What are you doing? Look, look, he's really close! Stop messing about with that.'

'Just enough to fill the pot, and can you please liquefy to flow .555 liquefaction, Jacob Crab, and shake 2.766 times while oscillating gently.'

'Jimmy!' Bibi shouted right in his ear. 'Have you gone totally loopy since your fall?'

♪ 'Jimmy's always been crazy ♬
♬ But not at all lazy ♪
♬ Often his plans are not that clear
♬ Until the very end of the year ♪
♪ But now we do need something really fantastic ♬

♬ OSM's coming fast and still swallowing plastic,' ♪

sang the Crab Gang from Zawn Cove while peering over the side at the fast-approaching monster Great Right Shark.

'Beautifully prepared, Jacob Crab, please to pour with care,' Captain Jimmy said in an other-worldly, calm voice. Bibi, all the time glancing back over her shoulder at the dark shape racing towards them, could only think that Captain Jimmy's brain cogs had finally totally disengaged and his mind had run right down like an old, broken clockwork toy.

'Sails. We must get the sails up, Jacob Crab. Now, let's do it now... fast!' Bibi ordered, thinking that their only chance now was for her to take command of the *Ocean Flyer* and to attempt to outrun OSM.

'Princess Liquorice, little mascot-y doggie, we need your super splendiferous flying skills for a secret zooming mission,' Captain Jimmy whispered into Liqc's ear while Bibi was busy sorting out which ropes to pull to set the sails. 'It's a very hush-hush, sausage-roll-reward mission. All that you have to do...' And he whispered silent instructions that Princess Liquorice was able to understand, because dogs can hear and understand vibrations. Princess Liquorice took off and circled the *Ocean Flyer* once before heading off.

Bibi shouted after her, 'This is no time for larking

around, and whatever are you playing at with that stupid yoghurt pot hanging from your collar?'

Captain Jimmy leapt backwards and up and down and sideways into frantic action. 'Bosun Jacob Crab, lower the flying hydrofoils, extend the balancing outriggers, hoist the sky zoom sails!' Captain Jimmy shouted orders as he madly pulled ropes, made critical sailing-speed adjustments, tangled his legs in loose ropes and fell back into the hole of broken floorboards and again emerged covered in Horrid Green Custard.

Spluttering, he looked up at Bibi, who was busy helping Jacob Crab madly hoist sails and said, 'Without waste of time entry to be made in ship's logbook to say, Previously Oscar Shark Friend has now become Oscar Shark enemy. He has grown hideously large, the size of a small island, and become wild with anger. The cause of this rapid and very weird growth to bigness unimaginable, it is suspected, is because of eating, ingesting plastic pollution particles and bits. We could be fleeing for our lives, beyond scared, with *Ocean Flyer* at max wide-open-jaw-escape racing speed. But Captain Jimmy the man has a plan to reach The Big Whizzo and thus, and to be completely sure to avoid gory ending.'

♬ 'No gory ending for us ♪
♬ Because that would be a terrible fuss ♬

♪ But how is it now possible to escape
♪ That terrifying razor toothed gape ♬
♬ Stinking breath already making our eyes sore
♪ Far better The Big Whizzo's welcoming roar,' ♬

'No time for logbook writing now, Jimmy!' Bibi frantically shouted. 'He's on us, he's got us, there's no escape!' But SnotTip had other ideas and finally wriggled out of Bibi's pocket. With a bad-tempered twist the ballpoint got unknotted, and, having spotted the logbook had spilled from Bibi's backpack in all of the commotion, made the entry as instructed by Captain Jimmy – with SnotTip additions.

While hauling on the mainsail halyard, Bibi took a quick fear glance towards the shark who was metres away. Princess Liquorice was hovering no more than two yoghurt pots' height above Oscar Shark Monster's nose.

'Get away, get away!' Bibi yelled at the top of her voice. 'Get away! You'll get sucked in!'

But then it happened. As he opened his enormous mouth ready to devour the entire *Ocean Flyer,* he stopped. He just stopped dead still in the water.

The sunlight glinted on a small green drop falling from the bottom of the yoghurt pot, hanging from Princess Liquorice's collar and splatting onto OSM's nose right beside his left nostril.

In the moment of calm that ensued, Bibi gathered up the ship's logbook, tied a very tight knot in SnotTip and shoved the logbook back into her backpack. SnotTip wriggled hard in her hand, and the logbook slipped back out of the backpack and opened its pages.

Quite exasperated by it all, Bibi snatched up the ship's logbook and was just about to snap it shut when SnotTip jiggled free from her grasp and slipped between the pages.

'What are you playing at, you stupid ballpoint?' Bibi was really getting annoyed. 'Are you two working together, by any chance?' Bibi said, while forcing the pages open to get SnotTip out. But before she could get a tight grip on the ballpoint, it had slipped back into her pocket.

As Bibi went to close the ship's logbook, she noticed a section of writing that had a green circle all around it:

*Sargasso Clingweed Rotation, 00.00 hours, Longitude West of West, Ocean Flyer and entire crew rescued by yoghurt pot dripping Horrid Green Custard onto Oscar Shark's nose.*

*Liquorice dog flying low, drip drip, drip... shark, HGC addicted, unable to resist Custard following drips to The Big Whizzo where flying dog instructed to head towards. Shark will clear path for Ocean Flyer through plastic*

*garbage to The Big Whizzo whirlpool.*
*All Horrid Green Custard will be delivered to Ocean Beyond mermaids so that they can add it to Mermaid Stones in attempt to clean up ocean plastic pollution.*
*PS. Body-knot-tying abuse makes the victim crazy angry and on the brittle edge of causing extensive damage.*

SnotTip had finished, so Bibi untied the knot, bent the troublesome ballpoint into a circle and stuffed it back into her pocket. She then gave Captain Jimmy a smacker of a kiss on his plastic cheek, even though he was again covered in glutinous HGC.

'Brilliant, brilliant, brilliant, not so dumb after all, you funny plasticky thing.' And then she gave him a hug, which, for the second time in his life, made him blush and for the first time in Bibi's life got her plastered in foul-tasting Horrid Green Custard. 'Does the yoghurt pot filled with HGC have a hole in the bottom? Is that how the drip works?'

'Precisely, precisely... Just the tiniest precision-hole-millimetre perfectly punctured by the very tip of Jacob Crab's claw,' Captain Jimmy confirmed, laughing unnaturally wildly.

'You really have come up with a great idea... Using the great mass of Oscar Shark Monster to swim through the plastic and weed and open a channel, like a great plastic breaker, that allows us to sail right through behind him to The Big Whizzo. Have you thought how angry he's going to be when he finds that he's been cheated?' Bibi laughed. 'Really, really angry when he finds that he's getting nothing but drips and that we are going to zoom past with the full cargo and all that he's had are tiny, tiny, drips. Wow is he going to be wild!'

♪ Oscar Shark Monster sure will be mad ♪
♬ When he finds its just drips he's had...that's sad ♬
♪ How big is The Big Whizzo, is what we're now asking ♬
♬ Can he squeeze into the whirlpool that's whizzing ♪
♪ Or can we zoom past him and sail right in ♬
♬ Laughing and singing and waving at him,' ♪

the Crab Gang sang.

Oscar Shark Monster's great bulk parted the floating plastic and left a wide clear channel for the *Ocean Flyer* to sail through. As he was only swimming slowly, at the speed that Princess Liquorice was flying, and teasingly dripping Horrid Green Custard, they quickly caught up with his lazily thrashing tail. Bibi waved to Princess Liquorice, but she was concentrating on getting the drips as close to his nostril as possible and was not looking back to see the wave.

'Not too close, Jimmy. OSM might get a whiff of the HGC that we have aboard and the floorboards have still not... Oh, I see,' she gasped, glancing down at the floor. 'I see that they have now. Another Just-in-the-Nick-of-Time job, I presume.'

Captain Jimmy did a very elegant bow.

It was all going to plan. Up ahead they could see the outer swirls of The Big Whizzo and that the plastic was thinning out enough to be able to sail without the aid of Oscar Shark Monster parting the pack plastic. It was all going to plan, and then it was not going to plan at all – the Horrid Green Custard in the yoghurt container ran out and the teasing drips stopped dripping.

Oscar Shark Monster thrashed his tail in annoyance. Then he crashed down on the pack plastic with his grotesquely grotesque mutant tentacles sending plastic flying in a whirlwind cloud of flying bits and spray.

Oscar Shark Monster twisted his body and turned his head so that one great eye was able to see back, to see Princess Liquorice shooting off with the empty yoghurt pot and heading back to the *Ocean Flyer* at full flying-collar speed. He ducked his head down, swallowed a great shark gob full of water and plastic bits and then spat it out with a terrifyingly angry roaring bellow.

'There's a space, Jimmy!' Bibi yelled as the plastic fell all around them. 'There's a space we can get through, crack on sail, crack on speed.'

But Captain Jimmy had already spotted it and had wound the *Ocean Flyer*'s speed up to max. The gap between the monster shark and the pack plastic was narrow and was all the time closing back, but for the moment the gap was there.

'Faster, Jimmy, faster!' Bibi yelled above the roar of the massive crashing waves, flying spray and bubbling foam created by angry tail and tentacle thrashing. And there was the stink, the utterly unmentionable shark breath stinkiness of burping rotten gas, belching out like decomposing dragon poo. '*Faster! Faster! Faster!*'

♪ 'Swamped, chewed and drowned ♬
♬ *Ocean Flyer* crew swallowed and never found,' ♪

wailed the Crab Gang from Zawn Cove.

Right at the last milli-nano second, as Oscar Shark Monster was about to swallow the *Ocean Flyer* and crew in one enormous stinking gobble, Bibi tossed the very last slice of her mum's chocolate brownie right down Oscar Shark Monster's throat. As Oscar Shark Monster slammed his mouth shut to swallow the brownie, Captain Jimmy whizzed the *Ocean Flyer* right past his closed lips, under one of his freakish tentacle fin-like arms, and down along the side of his rough, shark spotted-skin body, right past the old long-healed rope wound that was red and bleeding because his skin had expanded so much when he had grown enormous.

'No, Jacob Crab!' Bibi yelled, horrified. 'Don't jump, don't'... But it was too late. He was already mid-air, not having noticed that Oscar Shark Monster had already taken the chocolate brownie bait, had for the moment shut his ugly, tooth-filled mouth, and that the *Ocean Flyer* had slipped under his tentacles.

It was a great, brave and heroic leap onto Oscar Shark Monster's back. He clung on and pinched the mightiest, hardest, meanest and most vicious pinch that he had ever, ever pinched in his entire crab life.

Oscar Shark Monster let out a terrifying howl-like roar, twisted and turned, rolled and wriggled in a desperate attempt to throw Jacob Crab off. Jacob Crab clung on and all the time pinched harder and harder with his fearsome giant claws.

The *Ocean Flyer* was being tossed and thrown around in the wild water as Oscar Shark Monster thrashed his great body in agony, desperately attempting to stop the pinching of those great claws by diving up and down into the dark, million fathoms deep ocean.

'The Big Whizzo directly ahead,' Captain Jimmy yelled above the foam and the fight and the awful constantly burping gassy toxic undigested plastic and other rotting stuff stink – but still, and against all odds, the brave crab hung on.

# - CHAPTER NINE -

## THE MIGHTY CRAB RESCUE

'We're not losing Jacob Crab. Sail around the top outer rim of The Big Whizzo, Captain Jimmy. We need time before we get sucked down in the centre whirlpool vortex!' Bibi screamed into the wind and flying spray. 'We will save him!' she cried, as she grabbed a length of rope and instructed Princess Liquorice to take the other end of the rope in her teeth and to, under no circumstances, mess around. 'Full power on the flying collar. Let's go, let's fly, let's save the Jacob Crab, even though he also has a terribly stupid liking for Horrid Green Custard. He's a hero and he's our hero!' Bibi screamed as she wrapped the rope around her wrist, thought '*massive rocket power boost*' and zoomed up high into the sky.

As they flew, the loop of rope hung between them. Bibi's plan was to fly low over Jacob Crab, for him to the grab the rope in a giant claw and for them to lift him up and out of the reach of Oscar Shark Monster's snapping jaws. Then, fly him back to the *Ocean Flyer* before it disappeared down The Big Whizzo – and that great ocean whirlpool, the entrance to the mermaid domain, now very close and already starting to suck the *Ocean Flyer* into its outer devilish swirl.

Princess Liquorice was flying in rollercoaster fashion. 'Quit that,' Bibi scolded. 'Fly straight. Look, there they are. Oscar Shark Monster's surfaced and look! Jacob Crab's still clinging on. Lower, let's go down lower.

'Jacob Crab!' Bibi shouted at the top of her voice. 'Up here, look up here!'

But Jacob Crab was unable to hear. He was just desperately clinging on for dear life. And then, without warning, Oscar Shark Monster dived again, and both shark and crab disappeared from sight into the five-mile deep Ocean Beyond.

'Go higher. Circle, circle around and keep a good lookout. We need to spot them as soon as they surface – crabs can't swim in deep water. If Jacob Crab loses his grip he'll sink miles down and drown.'

Princess Liqcs did a sneaky backflip thinking Bibi wasn't watching. 'I said quit that,' she scolded, catching sight of the move out of the corner of her eye.

'Woof woof woof,' Liqcs barked. 'Down there, over

there, towards the sun.'

They zoomed around, approached from behind and Princess Liquorice landed on the top of Jacob Crab's broad landing-pad-like carapace. 'Hi,' she barked, 'surprise, surprise!'

In total stunned shock, Jacob Crab released his tight grip on Oscar Shark Monster and started sliding down his grooved, spotted, rough-skinned shark body towards his wild and madly angry foam-thrashing tail.

'HERE! Take the rope,' barked Princess Liquorice desperately. 'Quick, quick, take it! We'll fly you up, up and up and up. Come on, you great shell-encased muscly moron that can't even bark, sniff or enjoy a good wee.'

Insulting Jacob Crab made him very angry. He grabbed hold of the hanging rope with a grim look of *just you wait* in his beady eyes. Princess Liquorice flew up to Bibi and gripped the rope tightly in her teeth.

'Max the power, Liqcs!' Bibi yelled. The rope went taught with the full weight of the giant crab suspended in the air. 'Max and double max the power, we need more height. He's only just above the waves and Oscar Shark Monster is circling, angry eyes bulging, ready to strike, breathing out clouds of foul smelling stick. Really think, *max max max*!'

Slowly, very slowly, they edged higher. Gradually,

very, very gradually, millimetre by millimetre, with boots and collar overheating and close to exploding, Bibi and Princess Liquorice hauled Jacob Crab out of reach of Oscar Shark Monster's massive gnashing, crab-crushing teeth and nauseating, suffocating stomach poo breath.

Captain Jimmy circling on the outer rim steered the *Ocean Flyer* right beneath Oscar Shark, and Bibi and Princess Liquorice dropped him down with a bang that smashed the newly just-in-the-nick-of-time repaired floorboards and smothered him in Horrid Green Custard. Jacob Crab, whose head was madly spinning anyway from his first-time flyer experience, believed that he must have arrived in pure green heaven.

# - CHAPTER TEN -

## DOWN THE BIG WHIZZO

Sitting on the side deck, wiping off splats of Horrid Green Custard, Bibi anxiously glanced back past Captain Jimmy who was standing with the steering tiller between his legs nonchalantly singing some of his own adapted words to *Heroes* by David Bowie and occasionally doing a bit of air guitar, distorting his lips to add drama.

'I will be king
And you can be queen
Though nothing will drive him away
We can beat him just for one day.'

'Hate to tell you this, Captain Jimmy Bowie, but he's looking angrier than ever and he's heading this way. Let's do The Big Whizzo thing before it's too late,' Bibi said, starting to get very anxious again.

Oscar Shark Monster was on the far side of the far rim of the kilometre-wide whirlpool surrounded by white water and flying bits of plastic, thrashing around in a frenzy of speed and anger.

Captain Jimmy turned to see where he was. 'Judging by the angle of the sun, the rotation speed of The Big Whizzo... Wednesday over Sunday squared... I estimate that, giving OSM a mean speed of two hundred and 73 miles per hour, he will be on us by summer bank holiday last year.'

'It's very lucky for us that you're so mathematically inclined, but just in case you're wrong by three hundred and 65 days I suggested that we do The Big Whizzo zooming down into the vortex thing – and we do it right now because, by my own non-mathematical calculations, he's just seconds away. *Just seconds* away.'

Bibi was right. It was true that the outer, gently inward-sloping rim of The Big Whizzo was wide, very wide, and it was also true that OSM could not cross the central downward sucking and roaring spinning vortex of plastic and spiralling water because it was too fast-turning and too tight in the centre. However, he was moving fast around the rim. Very fast around the rim. And was throwing up a great bow wave of foam and plastic as he raced around to attack again.

'Life jackets, Jacob Crab. Lifejackets, life rings and an inflatable duck ring for the doggie mascot-y thingy,' Captain Jimmy ordered, having belatedly noticed that his mathematical calculations concerning the time of arrival of OSM were critically, absolutely mad, and heading them all towards yet another total disaster. 'Everyone to fix and fasten and lash lifejacket, cords and tapes, and squeeze the Crab Gang from Zawn Cove into a Coke bottle, screw on the top and tie a rope to it, with less time to spare than there was before.'

'Have you ever been down The Big Whizzo before?' Bibi shouted above the increasing roar of water while donning her faded and torn cork and canvas, half-a-century-or-more-old lifejacket in the belief that anything was better than nothing, but doubting that it would help much in the biggest ocean whirlpool on the planet.

'It's whizzing terror,' Captain Jimmy laughed. 'Sails down, hydro zoopers up, ship the rudder, lower the mast, lash the spars, grip on to anything that won't break. But last time everything got smashed to smithereens anyway so no need to really bother about holding on too much as it's going to be matchwood. Ha, ha!'

'So, last time it ended up shipwrecked and in pieces?' Bibi grabbed Princess Liquorice, wrapped her in a lifejacket, tied rope around her a few times and then secured it around her own waist.

'I was in a dream bubble,' Captain Jimmy explained, as if any old normal was totally normal, and started singing *Heroes* and performing air guitar, but the *Ocean Flyer* was tilting hard and he lost his footing and slithered onto his bum back into the Horrid Green Custard.

He climbed out, slipped a lifebelt over his head and stood up, holding on tight to the foredeck edge, combing and grinning a bit manically like you do just before the really, really terrifying bit comes on a rollercoaster ride.

Bibi collapsed laughing nervous laughter. 'Jimmy, oh my goodness! Wherever did you get this life-saving equipment? It's very faded but it has RMS Titanic printed on yours. Is this stuff that you picked up from among the floating rubbish while I was away with Liqcs rescuing Jacob Crab? Do you know what happened to RMS Titanic?'

Captain Jimmy turned, smiled enigmatically, and then started waving and throwing kisses at particularly large pieces of rubbish as they zoomed past, all the time gathering speed going around and down.

'Probably a very silly question,' Bibi called out, 'but if we spiral down clockwise, when will The Big Whizzo reverse and allow us to spiral up and out anti-clockwise? Or am I being stupidly logical again?'

'When our big cheese is aligned with 2.25 million

alien big cheeses across the solar system and...' He broke off to toss a splodge of Horrid Green Custard onto a half-submerged shipping container gripped in the vortex wall of water with the sea-worn words '*20,000 plastic bath ducks*' stencilled on the side, as they zoomed past.

'So, not that often then,' Bibi laughed. 'Not that often that solar cheeses get that organised.'

Her phone rang, 'Hi, Dad. Yeah, doing brilliantly, thanks. And Liqcs is naughty as usual. What am I doing? It's a really long, long story. Tell you at the weekend when you get back, but it's exciting, really exciting... Yeah, no I'm not teasing. I know... Okay, tell you this bit ... It's called the Titanic Ride... Yeah, yeah, a sort of rollercoaster disaster... Is it FAST? Wow is it FAST! Fading out, bye, love you.'

A brief shadow passed over, causing Bibi to glance up. Way up above on the whirlpool's rim the dark shape of Oscar Shark Monster loomed briefly and then disappeared from sight.

'What if the solar cheeses melt and don't ever orbit into line? What then? Sort of cheese-on-Pluto or cheesy-hoops-around-Saturn instead of cheese-on-toast?' Bibi said, pulling the ship's logbook from her backpack and straightening out SnotTip.

'On Friday, Friday at teatime, every Friday?' Captain Jimmy replied, while saluting the weed-covered remains of a wrecked fishing boat. 'Always do, celestially guaranteed.'

'Celestially guaranteed,' Bibi repeated. 'Well, heavens above! No probs then!'

Speed was increasing, the angle getting steeper, the centrifugal force getting stronger and the gurgling roar building and building. Taking a daring peep over the side, Bibi saw dark, swirling water packed with plastic bits racing round and round and disappearing –

D-I-S-A-P-P-E-A-R-I-N-G.

'This is your last chance at glory, SnotTip,' Bibi said, straightening the ballpoint out, watching the ship's logbook open with a shiver and a tremble. In Bibi's hand, SnotTip raced from page to page scribbling copious notes; impatiently waiting for pages to turn before scribbling on. Some words or even sentences Bibi was able to snatch a look at.

*Hold on for your life! Now we're into The Big Whizzo, the maddest place on the planet... Whoever's stupid enough to spiral down a whirlpool in the centre of the ocean? Whoever is that crazy? This will end in a Titanic disaster... Captain Jimmy is plastic anyway, so what does he care? It's all plastic here everywhere... Uuugh!*

Bibi tried identifying different objects, counting them

and listing them in the ship's logbook as they spiralled down the biggest, fastest and absolutely the most scary bath plug on the planet – the planet ocean bath plug. Sand buckets, bottles, ropes and fishing buoys, wheels from a bike, coffee cups, fizzy drinks bottles, bottle tops of all colours by the thousand, disposable cigarette lighters...

But the swirling wall was getting steeper, so steep that the *Ocean Flyer* was right over on her side and the swirling wall was getting faster. Bibi was getting giddy. And the swirling wall was all the time getting louder and louder. Bibi had shoved the wriggling SnotTip back into the bottle, screwed down the top and tightened the string that attached it to her waist, all the time trying to cling tightly onto Princess Liquorice who was struggling to escape to see just what flying in a twisting, swirling, roaring and spinning ocean vortex was like.

Very faintly, above the watery sounds, from within the folds of canvas and cork prophetic, words could occasionally be heard, in odd lulls in the gurgle, from the Crab Gang:

♬ 'New on the menu at the chippy now ♬
♪ It's plastic and chips, how's that for a wow ♪
♪ Cod once flaky and white, is now a sad,
plasticky sight ♬

♬ And don't ask for haddock or you'll
get a terrible fright ♪
♬ What about a nice battered, nurdle-filled
Dover sole, sir? ♪
♪ Or would you prefer the toxic plaice of the year?' ♬

And then THUMP, BANG, CRASH! They had arrived on a pure white sand beach in a lavender-coloured lagoon with multicoloured palm trees and a scattering of very beautiful white crystal rocks.

# - CHAPTER ELEVEN -

## A ZOOPTING DISASTER

'Okay, okay, SnotTip. You are the most impatient flexi HGC ballpoint that I have ever known – right, the only one. But just stop jigging about. Everything's in a terrible tangle and I need to get clear from this rope and these sails... and this stupid cork life jacket... far more dangerous than not having one at all, if you ask me. SnotTip, stop it.' Bibi had always hated things to be messy and now she was in a super mess with rope and sails and masts and booms and a rudder and life jackets and a RMS Titanic life ring. Worse still, there was an upside-down giant crab jerking its claws about, and Horrid Green Custard converted back to barrels all over the place.

'Liquorice, absolutely no flying, and I really mean it,' she said firmly, right in her face and tapping her on the nose to add emphasis. 'No flying whatsoever – this place definitely looks like a dog no-fly zone.' Princess Liquorice growled defiantly. 'No flying, absolutely – didn't you know that all undersea mermaids have a very strict no dog-flying policy? SnotTip, you are driving me mad!'

But where was Captain Jimmy?

Bibi pushed the sail out of the way, leant over the side and peered around. 'What are you doing?' she exclaimed, totally bemused. 'Has this *vital* mission suddenly become a beach holiday?'

Captain Jimmy grinned. 'Chilling,' he said while sipping Horrid Green Custard from a slightly broken plastic cocktail glass, lounging on a barnacle-encrusted sunbed wearing a green, tatty plastic sun visor.

'Yes, SnotTip, ok I'll let you out, such a fuss about being sealed in a bottle – *it was for your own safety, you know*. Would you rather have been mixed up with the rest of the floating trash?' Bibi unscrewed the plastic Coke bottle.

SnotTip leapt out into her hand. The ship's logbook flicked open and the bad-tempered ballpoint wrote *GASP, GASP!* in block letters treble underlined.

Bibi laughed, 'I don't think so! But when you poor, nearly suffocated flexi ballpoint have got your breath back, then let's write an official description of the amazing Big Whizzo beach and lagoon... '*resort*' is it Captain Jimmy Ocean?' she called out across the beach.

'Where shall we start?'

*Imagine an Olympic-sized stadium but with rotating walls of water containing millions of kaleidoscopic pieces of plastic of every possible description, and remember that this great cavernous space is deep beneath the ocean, and that all of the water and plastic that has drifted from far off continents is held in position by centrifugal force – a rotating outward pushing force and magic. Above is The Big Whizzo entrance, maybe portal even, which spirals down from the Ocean Beyond surface; starting wide, sunlight sparkling on the racing water, rotating slowly at the ocean surface but getting tighter and faster until the pinkish glowing, very, very mystical and magic world of the mermaids is finally reached. Deep, deep down in a world never seen before by a human person's eyes... Except mine... Wow!*

Bibi paused writing with SnotTip, who appeared to be going through a good behaviour phase, and, having pushed Jacob Crab upright, extricated the Crab Gang from Zawn Cove from the ropes and bits, she stepped out onto the pristine sugar-like sand. The first thing that she did was to bend down, touch it carefully with her finger and taste a few granules in case it really was sugar. -

But it was neither sand nor sugar. It had a taste that she had never tasted before – it tasted of *starlight*.

'How weird is that,' she said to herself, 'for such a strange taste thought to come into my mind – *a starlight-tasting beach – get that!*'

Princess Liquorice jumped down beside her, took a few cautious steps and then had a wee on the sugar-like white beach sand.

'Liquorice!' Bibi scolded. But it had gone. Within a second the small patch of yellow wee had completely disappeared.

'How about that, is that weird or what?'

When you have billions of litres of seawater containing billions of bits of plastic whizzing around at super high speed, forming an enormous cavern beneath the ocean, then would you not expect it to be noisy? Deafeningly noisy, in fact, Bibi said to herself. But not only was there no sound at all, it was like being in a place of negative sound – sort of sound minus.

And when she looked back there were no footprints. Captain Jimmy still lounging on his lounger, still laid back on the sharp barnacles and '*chilling*' with dedication, had also managed to get ten metres from the beached *Ocean Flyer* without the trace of a trainer footprint impression remaining in the sugar/sand.

Princess Liquorice did a little hover. 'I said, NO,' hissed Bibi, waving her down.

Just at that moment, just when Bibi was experimenting with making footprints and watching them immediately disappear, seven glistening silver-scaled mermaids emerged from the lavender pinky-coloured lagoon, sat on the milky crystal rocks and ran their fingers through their long tresses of fluorescent green hair.

Bibi just grinned. 'Now isn't that amazing? Wowee! Real mermaids.' But suddenly having a doubt, a doubt about it all, she turned to Captain Jimmy. 'This isn't one of your tricks, is it? Some sort of VR illusion? Don't tell me it is because I really do want to meet real mermaids.'

A selfie with seven mermaids! Now that really would impress Dad – Mum would want ironclad proof that they existed, of course, and the Spanish cousins would just burn up in flames of jealousy, hurrah!'

Captain Jimmy put down his HGC cocktail and called out to the mermaids, 'We have the magic ingredient – the Horrid Green Custard – for the undersea ocean factory of plastic transformation. Barrels and barrels of it all ready to be loaded onto Zippy. Is he awake yet?'

The mermaids whooped and cheered – one put two fins in her mouth and whistled with a whistle so piercing that it very nearly stopped the plasticky garbage bits spinning in the watery walls.

'We'll get someone to jerk his tentacle. Zippy is sooo

lazy,' one of the mermaids sang out and laughed.

'Impressive mermaids,' thought Bibi to herself as she crunched across the beach towards where they were sitting, giving a little tentative wave as she went, not too sure how mermaids viewed human people or dogs with attitude who could fly, come to that.

Liquorice was scampering around sniffing. Bibi was thankful that she was not doing any show-off flying, although she feared that it could happen any second – and that would be *totally* embarrassing!

But Princess Liquorice was not able to resist doing a long, slow wee right in front of the mermaids on the clear crystal rock. And while she was doing it, she stared up at Bibi and gave her a very serious you-shouldn't-have-stopped-me-flying smile. The only disappointing thing about the defiant wee, as far as Princess Liquorice was concerned, was that all trace disappeared virtually before it showed.

Bibi felt a bit nervous. Normally she never felt nervous. Even in her old school, whenever she had to perform in front of the whole school, in a play or to talk on stage about the Pharaohs, which she once did, she was never nervous – but of course, perhaps mermaids, deep under the ocean in their own very extraordinary space could be considered a bit different to school assembly hall. Some might even say scarier.

'My name is Bibi Lopez-Miller and this is Princess Liquorice Lopez-Miller. Which language do you speak, if indeed you speak any human language at all?' Bibi asked hesitatingly.

'I speak the language that you speak when I am speaking to you, and I speak the language that the water speaks when I am speaking to the water, or the language that the rocks speak when I am speaking to the rocks,' one of the mermaids smiled with a smile that positively glowed. 'My name is Lavendoria and I would like to introduce the six Izzys: Izzy Luna, Izzy O, Izzy Peach, Izzy $H_2O$, Izzy Wonder and Izzy Brains. We have heard so much about you and your life from Plastic Jimmy, and we have all been so looking forward to meeting you. Can I offer you a sticky bun?'

'Is it one of Granny Bluebell's? Bibi laughed a bit nervously in total disbelief. She had thought that with all she had already been through since leaving Playing Place Cove that nothing could ever shock her again... *But a Granny Bluebell's shop beneath the Ocean Beyond!!!!*

'It is indeed,' Lavendoria confirmed with very kind and knowing smile.

Princess Liquorice barked, 'There's weird and there's weird - but this is just getting too weird. Granny Bluebell's sticky buns here, under the ocean – are you insane? And I suppose you have Granny Bluebell's sausage rolls too!'

Bibi was about to interpret Liqc's bark when Lavendoria nodded with a smile. 'Yes, I understand, Princess Liquorice, and yes, Princess Liquorice, I do have Granny Bluebell's sausage rolls, because we know that Granny Bluebell's sausage rolls are your favourite treat – slightly warmed as you like them.'

'Well, gobble my tongue down,' Liqcs growled happily, swallowing the magic sausage roll in one greedy gulp.

'We have heard a lot about you as well, Princess Liquorice. We know that you are funny and naughty sometimes, and that you get very hot in the summer and like to splash in the waves. We love that too, especially Izzy $H_2O$ – playing in waves is her special treat. I expect that you find that funny as we're mermaids and in the sea all of the time, but that's just it – we're in the sea but only rarely on the beach in the waves breaking on the sand... and that is such fun. Oh, I wish we could do it now, don't you girls? Sometimes the dolphins and porpoises play in the waves with us too... Hey, wild surfing is awesome!'

Princess Liquorice started to growl menacingly. Bibi turned to see what the trouble was. 'Oh my dog, what's that? It's not... is it? I mean... Oh no, is it Oscar Shark Monster?'

A very large creature was slowly, very slowly, emerging from the lavender-coloured lagoon, doing so without making the slightest ripple or stir.

'That's not Oscar Shark, that's Zippy Squid; the biggest and the slowest squid in the oceans,' Izzy Luna laughed.

'But he is an all-terrain amphibious squid,' explained Izzy Brains, clearly something of an authority on squid.

'He's a multiple-tentacle all-terrain squid,' explained Izzy Wonder.

'And he is strong,' Izzy O pushed a bit to the front to explain.

'But he's not Oscar Shark. He's mean, but Zippy Squid is just slow and lazy,' laughed Izzy Peach, 'slow and lazy.'

'We are aware of the terrible Oscar Shark mutant growth situation,' said Izzy Brains, 'and we are working on a solution to ocean plastic toxicity and the disastrous consequences for marine life in general – but, of course, Oscar Shark is a particular concern.'

'I call Oscar Shark, Oscar Shark Monster because he's grown so enormous and become very, very nasty and angry. Jacob Crab told me that he used to be Jimmy's friend, but he's not anymore,' Bibi said.

'That is a useful update.' Izzy Brains nodded and smiled.

'Jimmy's friend, ha ha! Jimmy's got a friend.' The other mermaids laughed, prodding each other with their fins as if it was the greatest joke imaginable.

'Well, I'm his friend,' said Izzy Peach. 'Yes, I'm Plastic

Jimmy's friend. And I don't mind saying so.'

'Well, that's because you fancy him,' all of the mermaids said chattering together, except for Izzy Brains who looked as if she was recording notes into what to Bibi looked like nothing more than a bubble.

'No, I do not,' protested Izzy Peach, looking coy in front of the other mermaids. But Bibi thought that she caught another sneaky look, a rather cold and mean look, and she wondered what that could mean and if the mermaids were all that they appeared on the smiley, lovely, surface.

'I just like him. He's different. What's wrong with that? And I agree with Bibi. He really is smarter than other sea creatures think... In fact, I think that he might just be a genius. So there, that's what I think. And that's down to Izzy Brains' years of research into *plastic zoopting. W*e all know how hard she works at that – *night and day.*'

'What's *plastic zoopting*?' Bibi asked, quite intrigued by the smiley – smiley or were they bitchy? – bitchy mermaids. 'I've never heard of that.' Her eyes were going from one to another carefully watching for any clues.

'Very simply put in laymaid's terms,' Izzy Brains said, squeezing her recording bubble into a small hidden pouch under one of her waist scales.

'Look at her tiny waist, girls. I wish I could tuck a recorder into my scales with not even the smallest bulge showing,' Izzy Peach remarked with a little twisty wriggle of her fins.

'I am very careful what I eat, you know, Izzy Peach. Well, anyway, to get back to Bibi's question. Toxins enter the marine food chain at the lowest zooplankton level, and small marine creatures eat plankton. Larger creatures eat smaller ones all the way up the chain to the top – whales, sharks and big fish – where toxic plastic zoopting, poison concentration, in larger marine creatures takes place and Great Right Sharks for instance, like Oscar Shark become 'zoopted'. That is, they change beyond all recognition – they mutate, possibly into monster marine creatures that are hardly recognisable even by their own species.'

'With your help, together with our research team, led by Izzy Brains and Prof Gilbert Octopus, not to mention the magical Horrid Green Custard, our plan is to de-zoopt all zoopted creatures and then to prevent it happening in the future,' Lavendoria explained.

'*My help?*' Bibi gasped, slightly taken aback and not at all sure if she should be delighted to be involved, honoured to be asked or even scared that they might have plans to zoopt her as an experiment. She had to admit that she did find Izzy Brains a bit on the scary side – somehow they all were, but in different ways.

'Oh yes, we have some amazing plans, and without your

help we will never be able to make them work,' Lavendoria explained. 'But can we talk about that later when we've shown you around and you've seen our amazing, highly advanced, I say modestly of course, undersea world? But there is one question that I wanted to ask now. Have you noticed how Plastic Jimmy, oh, I'm sorry Captain Jimmy Ocean,' (hearing that made the mermaids giggle a bit). 'Have you noticed how strangely he's acting?'

'I've not known him long. He certainly is odd but, after all, he is *plastic*.' Bibi was a bit thrown by the question. 'I mean,' she asked herself, 'is an illusion odd? Or is an illusion just an illusion and that's the end of it, and what a strange thing for talking mermaids to be asking anyway.'

'Well, look at him now. Not even helping Jacob Crab load the barrels of Horrid Green Custard into Zippy Squid's multiple-tentacle grasp. Just sipping his cocktail of HGC and grinning like he's gone a bit soft in the head. I think that I'll have to get Professor Gilbert Octopus or Izzy Brains to have a look at him. Maybe he needs a service or an upgrade. And he's not even come to say hello... Not even come to give Izzy Peach a kiss,' Lavendoria laughed and all of the other mermaids laughed too, except Izzy O who pouted and looked the other way.

'He plans things, maybe that's what he's doing now; planning his next move. And he does have moments that are more lucid than others,' Bibi elaborated, sort of thinking aloud.

'You're right. Plastic Jimmy is Plastic Jimmy after all, but we must get his word selection sorted out, Izzy Brains. It does go a bit wonky sometimes. Of course, it might just be too much of that latest brew of Horrid Green Custard, and I've heard it's an extra strong batch. Have you noticed that, Bibi my dear, the odd way that he puts words together?' Lavendoria asked.

'But it always makes sense in its weird way. Sometimes more than just making sense. It's sometimes really clever – profound, even,' Bibi explained, realising that actually she felt quite close to Captain Jimmy – it must be because of their recent adventures together, or was it more? Had he, in a very strange way, become the brother that she missed having? Quite weird, she found herself thinking – a plastic boy, or was he mysteriously more than that, was he really an oddball plastic genius – was that the way that Izzy Peach saw him? Was that what Izzy Brains and Prof Gilbert Octopus had created?

'Sounds like Izzy Peach is going to need to watch out. Sounds like our Plastic Jimmy has another secret admirer,' teased Izzy Luna laughing like mad.

Bibi took a selfie while all of the mermaids were laughing and showed it to them.

'Oh goodness! My hair's such a mess... Just look at my roots!' exclaimed Izzy Wonder, running her fingers through her florescent green tresses.

The six Izzys dived from the crystal rock into the glowing lagoon; Lavendoria followed without the tiniest, weeniest splash.

Bibi looked around, looked at Princess Liquorice who had broken all the rules and promises and was flying around skimming low over the sugar/sand but she had more to think about than what Liqcs was doing.

While she was mulling over her first encounter with mermaids, Bibi sent the mermaid selfie to her dad. There would be time later to send it to her mum. She knew that her dad would laugh but was pretty sure that her mum would ask masses and masses of very difficult questions and could very easily get very cross that she was not being as careful as she had promised to be. Even worse, the mermaid selfie might even result in her being grounded.

Bibi was very thoughtful as she walked along the edge of the lagoon back towards the beached *Ocean Flyer*. Zippy Squid had loaded up with Horrid Green Custard and had very slowly slipped back into the depths of the lagoon with his cargo. Jacob Crab was asleep and probably dreaming about the good old days when rockpools were rockpools, sand was real sand and water was not lavender coloured –

if indeed the lagoon was even water at all.

Princess Liquorice had lost all care about being told off and was far away, flying close to the outer wall of spinning water and plastic. Bibi watched her for a while and then whistled for her to come; worried that she might, in her mad way, go too close to the rushing water and bits and get sucked in. In the strange silence of the silent Big Whizzo, her whistle was so loud that when it hit Princess Liquorice she flipped upside down and nearly flew headlong into a kid's broken plastic bike.

Bibi put her hand over her mouth in horror but Princess Liquorice quickly righted herself, gave herself a good shake and barked back. The bark in turn blew Bibi's hair out straight like a gale of wind.

Something about the mermaids made her feel uneasy, but she was not able to put a finger on what it was. She was just having a smile to herself about the mermaids calling Captain Jimmy Ocean 'Plastic Jimmy' when Lavendoria popped her head up above the '*water substance*' and said, in a hushed voice dripping with mystery, 'Would you like to follow me? I have loads to show you in The Wonder.'

'Shall we swim or fly?' Bibi called out, totally bemused, over '*the water substance*' to Lavendoria who was swimming around without a ripple to be seen.

'Oh, you can walk. It's not far, and it's perfectly safe

– it's only water!' Lavendoria replied, with a smile which seemed to Bibi to say *'you can be a bit silly at times, human creature.'*

'Silly me,' Bibi muttered under her breath. 'It's only '*water*' after all – which is normally quite sinky stuff when human creatures walk on it in the other world.'

'Go and stir Jimmy Plastic from his sun bed; he's a *genius*,' she laughed, 'and anyway he's been there. The Wonder was where he was created, if he can get his plastic cogs working to remember.' She laughed again and disappeared.

The Crab Gang from Zawn Cove cautiously plopped one at a time from the deck of the *Ocean Flyer* to the dazzling sand, and then, in short darting bursts, they went towards '*the substance*' water.

♬♪ 'If you swim in it, it lets you in ♪
♪ Or you can walk on it, which makes you grin ♪
♪ Is it for eating, will it freeze into ice? ♬
♬ We all think it scary, and not very nice ♪
♬ What's wrong with water, simple and clear ♬
♪ Why do we need something new, that's
probably ever so dear,' ♬

sang the Crab Gang poking '*the substance*' with extreme trepidation.

Fearless Princess Liquorice was the first to venture onto the surface proper. She hovered for a few moments and then she landed on the surface of the lavender lagoon '*water substance*'.

'Hey, look at this, Bibi,' she called back. 'I can stand. It's not '*water*,' it's not glass – in a way, it's sort of not anything. It's not anything but it's there and it moves, it has a colour and it's... just amazingly *weird*! WOW*!*'

''Tis dimensionless,' announced Jacob Crab with giant crab-like authority, as he had a scientific interest in all forms of water, gloop, Horrid Green things and generally all things down right weird.

Without warning, Captain Jimmy jumped up from his sun bed. He strode out across the lavender-coloured lagoon '*substance*', scanning the horizon with his brass telescope, taking a compass bearing to the geophysical centre of the lagoon and announcing decisively, 'Right, here we have it. Everyone to me.'

SnotTip was not convinced. SnotTip wriggled and turned until it was out of Bibi's pocket and writing on the palm of Bibi's hand:

*Mermaids are slippery.*

'You're beginning to annoy me, you wriggly green

streak ballpoint punk,' Bibi said crossly as she folded the ballpoint into a Z and stuffed it back into her pocket. But out it popped again, behaving in a very SnotTippy way, that is to say zippy, angry and altogether bad pen-nasty. SnotTip flipped out of Bibi's hand and onto *'the substance'* surface. Bibi bent down but as she took hold of the pen it was as if SnotTip grabbed her hand, pulled her down and made her write – WobbleGumph in *'the substance'* which almost instantly disappeared.

'Genius,' Bibi exclaimed. 'Pure genius. SnotTip, considering that you're totally stupid .... that's genius! Jimmy!' Bibi called out 'WobbleGumph, that's what I'm going to call it. You call it that boring old *'the subtance'* name, but we're calling it WobbleGumph, much more exciting....Brilliant job, you stupid genius,' Bibi said, giving SnotTip a quick kiss before returning the pen to her pocket where she could feel SnotTip doing little show off shimmies of pride.

But it was not actually the WobbleGumph that was bothering her, nor the fact that she had not yet had a reply from Dad. It was what Lavendoria had said about needing her to help on the project.

It might be important, really, really important. Before the voyage had really started, Captain Jimmy had said that it was *vital*, but it was a question of time. How much spare time did she have, she asked herself, what with adventures and writing down all of the details about them. All of the home schooling that was endless and getting worse as she got older, walking Princess Liquorice, reading (which took a lot of her time) computer gaming and social media stuff, visiting Lucy and Tom, her friends at the farm, running endless errands around the village for the 'oldies'. Not to mention being semi-official sticky-bun taster for the Granny Bluebell shop/organisation, or even global empire as it seemed to be expanding into – well, what time was there for a *vital* project?

Bibi had just about made up her mind to tell Lavendoria that it was very kind of her to make the offer, but she would have to say no, when her phone pinged with a message alert. She expected it to be a reply from her dad, and was disappointed when she saw that it was from OSM and just said BLOCKED but with a gruesome-looking shark emoji added for scary effect.

'OSM,' she said to herself and then out loud, 'O... S... M, not that Oscar Shark Monster... Whatever is happening here? This is all going really screwy. How can he be sending *me* messages? He's A SHARK!'

Yanking SnotTip from her pocket, Bibi wrote on her hand, 'What do you know about this? Is this your doing? You think this is some sort of joke?'

SnotTip gave a ballpoint shrug and replied:

*Told you, mermaids are slippery.'*
*'All of them?'*
*'What, you think I'm a snitch?*
*'No, you're a NIGHTMARE!'*

# - CHAPTER TWELVE -

## PURPLE SPIRAL TO WONDER

Captain Jimmy Ocean looked totally ridiculous. He was walking on tiptoes while reading his compass, holding his right arm, which was made out of plasticky bits, high in the air while whistling *'A life on the Ocean Wave'* for what seemed like no reason at all. On his feet he had on a pair of retro red-and-white trainers, which were somehow many sizes too big for him on the outside, but, like Bibi's flying boots, appeared to fit perfectly. Emanating from the bulbous white toe was a white glow, which shone down into the *'water'*.

'Cool trainers,' Bibi called out. 'Were they washed down or did you just-in-the-nick-of-time make them?'

Captain Jimmy waved his raised arm to indicate that he was concentrating and was not to be disturbed... under any circumstances.

'So what if?' Bibi was talking to herself while watching

Captain Jimmy tiptoeing around like a demented ballerina in oversized, *although super cool*, glow-worm trainers. 'What if... Oscar Shark Monster and the mermaids are secretly working together on some sneaky or even some monstrously evil plan, and it's the mermaids or at least one of the mermaids sending scary OSM messages and particularly nasty big-teethed shark emojis on her phone? No, no, no. That's all too daft. It's all Big Whizzo, parallel worlds, plastic captains, oversized this and that and singing crabs – madness!' Bibi laughed at herself. What we need here is a bit of real-world sanity and to stop listening to stupid, interfering, flexi HGC ballpoint pens. That will help. Get a grip, Bibi,' she chided herself.

'Have you found what you're looking for, Captain Jimmy?' she called out across the lagoon.

'YES! YES! YES!' Jimmy yelled. 'Got it, got it exactly!' His yell zoomed round and round the outer whizzing water wall, skidded over the surface of the lavender lagoon and hit Bibi full force, plopping her down hard onto her skinny little bottom.

'Ouch! Just be careful!' she purposely whispered, so as not to get any more sound blasts. She got to her feet and stared at the spooky way that the WobbleGumph was rapidly changing colour right beneath Captain Jimmy's super cool trainers. 'Jimmy, look down.' She mouthed the words while she walked across the lagoon to where he was standing, gazing around and absent-mindedly grinning.

The white light from his trainers was glowing purple in the WobbleGumph and intensifying and expanding dramatically into an enormous downward spiral of brilliant purple light, illuminating the depths.

Bibi arrived at his side. 'Jimmy, look down, under your feet look,' she said in awe.

Captain Jimmy immediately did a handstand, balanced perfectly on his hands and exclaimed excitedly, 'There it is! I knew that I could locate it directionally and by mathematical reasoning. It's the portal to The Wonder.'

'Put your feet down; it's dimming a bit,' Bibi instructed. 'It seems to need the light source from your trainers to excite the intense purple spiral of deep light.'

The spirally glow of purple reached a long, long way down, and in the depths, moving fast upwards along the twists of the spirals, two mermaids were racing each other to the surface.

'I was first,' gasped Izzy $H_2O$.

'No, I was first. I won, I won!' said Izzy Peach.

'You cheated anyway; you pushed me,' complained Izzy $H_2O$

'No, I did not. You started before I said GO, and that's not fair. I was first, wasn't I Bibi?' Izzy Peach winked one of her large peachy eyes. 'Say I was, because, because, because...'

'Because what? You're such a cheat! You always cheat all of the time,' Izzy $H_2O$ said, getting really exasperated. '*Because what,* what are you trying to do? Make Bibi cheat too? Be in on your cheating side, is that it? We all know what you're like, sneaky Peach, sneaky Peach.'

'Looked equal to me. What did you think, Captain Jimmy?' Bibi asked. 'Jacob Crab, did you see who won?'

♬♪ 'It's a funny thing when first you dream,
of being fast and furious ♪
♪ We once knew a crab who was always last ♬♪
♬♪And he was the one that laughed and laughed ♪
♬♪ What made him so happy, to some might
be a bit curious,' ♬

sang the Crab Gang.

'We will all race down to The Wonder,' Captain Jimmy announced, 'all in a line around the circle.'

'That sounds daft to me. You mean, everyone forms a circle around the purple portal to The Wonder, which is only a glowing light beneath your trainers and not an entrance or anything like a way in, to whatever is below... Well, it's all daft.' Bibi was getting a bit fed up with the mermaid bickering, the whole weird set-up and not receiving a reply from her dad.

'That's exactly what I said and I could not have explained it better and I will be the winner, so there,' Captain Jimmy said, bending in a diving posture with hands and arms pointing down. 'One, two, three and on to the total blackness of the eclipse, GO!'

'Ok, let's do it,' Bibi sighed, getting really fed up with swimming against the current of craziness. Well, what could go wrong?

After that she was *standing* on a firm substance called WobbleGumph that was also meant to be water because, after all, the mermaids had just swum up through it. It was possible, Bibi considered, that it was not so firm where the purple light was, but it certainly appeared to be the same consistency because it was bearing Captain Jimmy and Jacob Crab's weights without any sign at all of softness... So what could possibly go wrong? Because diving into glass that's meant to be water had to be the same as diving into water that just happens to have the feel and appearance of glass. 'Now that's just common sense, isn't it,' Bibi said to herself. 'You go first Captain Jimmy. After all, your head's made of plastic.'

But before Plastic Jimmy dived, the two mermaids jostling with each other disappeared into the purple. Bibi was just totally amazed; they just dived into a solid, and spiralled away down into the purple glowing depths. Captain Jimmy followed. Princess Liquorice flew high into the air, bombed in and barrel-rolled all of the way down. Jacob Crab with the Crab Gang on his broad carapace slipped in sideways.

'Well, all of the others are as mad as hatters, so why not?' Bibi jumped into the purple twisting water WobbleGumph slide and zoomed down twisting round and round until she stopped where all of the others had stopped. It was not perhaps what you would normally call the bottom, or the floor or anything like that. It was just a stopping place.

The thing was, they were still all in the WobbleGumph, a substance that was all things at once. You could walk on it, swim and slide in it and at the same time you could breathe in it.

Captain Jimmy helped Bibi to her feet.

'Yes, it is odd,' Bibi remarked looking around, and whispered in Captain Jimmy's ear, 'Are all of the mermaids to be trusted, do you think? And how do we get home from here? That is, of course, my home that I'm talking about because I imagine this is what you more or less call your home.' And then, as an afterthought, she added quite casually, 'Are me and Princess Liquorice hostages or perhaps prisoners? And just out of passing interest, what exactly do mermaids eat?'

♬♪ 'Portal Slide, dream and ride ♬
♪ Into wet water and coming out dried ♬♪
♪ Sliding like greased lightening ♪
♬ 'Awesome,' says Jacob Crab, but frightening – and very enlightening' ♪

'Welcome to The Wonder,' said Lavendoria. 'Please follow me. It really is so exciting for all of us that you're here at last. Here, let me open the Colour for you.'

'Thank you, but what does that mean?' Bibi was busy looking around and was very aware of SnotTip jerking around angrily.

'In '*the substance*' we don't have physical doors.' Izzy Brains slipped in from another Colour to explain. 'But we do have rooms, or perhaps compartments, and they are all different colours, and to pass from one to another we simply open a Colour and go in. So please, after you.'

Captain Jimmy went into the wrong Colour and took a moment to find his way back, opening and closing Colours this way and that. 'Fortunately, I'm not colour blind in the ears,' Bibi heard him muttering, and laughed.

Princess Liquorice flew up to whisper in Bibi's ear. 'You know that I wee-ed on the white sand and it disappeared? Well, the thing is, well it's like this, and well...'

'Oh, get on with it,' Bibi hissed back. 'And just you keep

still, SnotTip.'

'The thing is, if I wee in this '*substance*' or WobbleGumph stuff, will I be flying around in wee after and breathing it in, or even worse swallowing it? And then there's a Colour question.'

'Which is?'

'Which Colour would be the best to wee in, or is there a specific loo Colour? If you ask me, it's a bit scary down here – no grass, no trees and not even the slightest sniff of a rabbit. Can we go soon?' Princess Liquorice growled very quietly, the sort of growl that Bibi knew was her '*I'm scared growl*', so she gave her a big hug.

'We will. Anyway, we have to be back for supper. I'll give Mum a call in a minute. Let's just see what's in this next Colour. And try not to wee, I hate to think what might happen.'

Izzy Wonder appeared and opened a Colour. Inside the Colour there were at least *ten thousand* octopuses busy sorting plasticky bits into individual bins. They were working away in a vast undersea cavern of a pinkish colour with an enormous collector device harvesting plastic garbage from the spinning walls.

'The Great Octopus Octo-Plastic Recycling Factory,' Captain Jimmy announced, throwing his arms into the air and darting back and forth, throwing open one Colour after another in a frenzy of random Colour slamming as if he just needed to let off steam.

'Jimmy, Jimmy, calm down. What's the problem?' Bibi asked, grabbing his arm and stopping him.

'It's his periphery gland that has been over stimulated,' Izzy Brains announced, pushing one of his eyelids up and then the other. 'All of those HGC cocktails, I feared they were too potent for his plastic. It'll probably wear off – I might have to get Prof Gilbert Octopus to give him a shot of toopoozin.'

When Izzy had gone into another Colour, Captain Jimmy moved towards Bibi until they were nose to nose. 'We might have to get out of here,' he whispered very, very quietly, while tweaking her ear lobe. 'Things are not how they used to be before they changed,' he warned nervously, flicking his eyes this way and that.

'Let me show you around,' Izzy Peach said sweetly, mysteriously appearing through a Colour. 'There's lots to see. We have so much happening here and a few secrets too,' she said very quietly and nodding knowingly. You don't need to come with us if you're busy, Plastic Jimmy. We girls have lots to talk about.'

Izzy Peach guided Bibi into an eerie pinkish-mauve Colour.

Bibi gasped, 'Oh my dog, just look at that. OMD that

is so unbelievable – so amazing or what?'

The Colour was vast. It was a sort of undersea factory like no other that exists, and in it there were thousands upon thousands of octopuses, and they were literally on each other, in an enormous tangle of tentacles, as big as the area of a football pitch. They were busy slithering back and forth over each other collecting and sorting the plastic that was whizzing down The Big Whizzo, collecting and binning, sorting and munching into very small pieces ready for octo-recycling.

'And what exactly is octo-recycling?' Bibi asked, her eyes still out on stalks in utter amazement.

'It's all a bit hush-hush,' Izzy Peach winked one of her big peachy mermaid eyes, 'but this much I can tell you. You know the beach beside the lagoon?'

'The crunchy white beach with sand-like sugar where footprints disappear?' Bibi asked.

'Yes, exactly! Izzy Peach exclaimed excitedly. 'Well after the chewed-up plastic goes through the Momentous Change Fusion Reaction Zupper Zapper in Reverse, that's how it comes out. And then... Well, this is very secret and I have been sworn to secrecy, as have we all down in The Big Whizzo. But if I whisper and if you promise never ever to say anything to anyone even if they squeeze and pinch you and do nasty things to try to make you talk, you'll have to cross-your-heart-and-hope-to die promise.'

'I promise,' Bibi said, intrigued to know any secret of the amazing mermaid undersea world.

'Well, one day, and quite by accident, the Momentous Change Fusion Reaction Zupper Zapper instead of running in reverse, reversed the reverse and amazingly, would you believe what was Zupper Zapped out? World changing and astounding '*the*...'

'This doggie is naughty,' Lavendoria burst through the Colour holding the hovering Princess Liquorice by the scruff of her flying collar. 'She has been trying to sniff out Granny Bluebell's sausage rolls, causing havoc in the Jellyfish Laboratory Colour. Absolute havoc.' Lavendoria gave her a final shake and passed her to Bibi.

'That's so bad. Why do I have to keep telling you to behave?' Bibi scolded and tapped her nose – the one thing that Princess Liquorice particularly hated.

Smiling sweetly, Lavendoria said, 'Princess Liquorice is such a lovely doggie but so naughty. It's the jellyfish, you see. They get very disturbed, and we are on the edge of a big scientific breakthrough moment, and they've never seen a flying doggie before, let alone such a naughty one as this little terrier who's into everything and dive bombing.'

Princess Liquorice licked Bibi's cheek and ear as if to say sorry, but really to say, in an almost imperceptibly low growl, 'we need to escape, don't let on, act normally...'

Bibi felt a cold shudder of fear run through her body. Captain Jimmy had warned her that something was wrong, and where was he now? SnotTip had nagged on about it, written *'mermaids are slippery'* but was SnotTip to be listened to or could a flexi ballpoint be relied upon to be a good source of credible info? Anyway, mermaids are sort of slippery by their very nature because they have scales and fish tails. But now Princess Liquorice had picked up on something that was wrong, and she had very well-tuned doggie senses for danger, and Princess Liquorice was totally loyal and could be one hundred percent trusted.

How do you escape from a parallel world? How do you get out of a dream that might be a nightmare? How do you find your way out of the WobbleGumph or The Big Whizzo or get back to Playing Place Cove, to Mum, to home, to your own really lovely bedroom with its own cherry-tree way of sneaking in and out of, all the way from the Ocean Beyond? Was escape possible? She had been seeking adventure, playing on her own and fantasising a bit, but what had she got into? Was it an adventure from which there was no escape? No escape at all?

Bibi was glancing around the very weird Octo-Plastic Recycling Plant pretending to be relaxed while trying to remember the route that they had travelled. Down The Big

Whizzo to the white beach was easy to remember, down the purple spiral through the WobbleGumph was clear in her mind although very peculiar, but the Colours, the maze of coloured chambers within the WobbleGumph were totally impossible to fathom.

She had absolutely no idea which way was north or south, up or down, or the way back to the purple spiral for a start. It was as if the mermaids had brought her into the WobbleGumph, a claustrophobic maze of coloured chambers which were totally without reference points, with the very intention of totally and completely and absolutely disorientating her. And they had, and she was, and it was very, very scary.

Out of the corner of her eye, Bibi glanced at Izzy Peach. She was standing on her wide-tail fin, absent-mindedly running her long thin fingers through her fluorescent turquoise tresses – looking as if she was miles away in her thoughts. All of the octopuses in the Octo- Recycling Plant were busy, tied up by tentacles even, in their own plastic sorting and munching world.

Nodding to Princess Liquorice to follow her, Bibi took the opportunity to slip through into another Colour, hoping that Izzy Peach was too involved with her own appearance to notice which way she had gone.

She had made the decision – she was going to find a

way out, she was going to find a way home. 'Nothing is impossible,' she said to herself in a very determined way. 'Nothing is impossible when you put your mind to it, whatever the difficulties, or whatever the danger – we can do it Liqcs, we can escape from this mermaid madness.'

The new chamber that they entered was pale blue and was empty. What she needed was to discover a sense of direction. 'Liqcs, which way to the purple spiral, can we fly, and can we fly back up it through the WobbleGumph? You've been flying in it and it's obviously thicker than air, so do you lose power?'

'This way,' Princess Liquorice growled very quietly. 'And fly low.'

The next chamber was dark blue and was also empty, but the chamber after was a total shock and Bibi flipped over Princess Liquorice and landed flat on the floor. The chamber was pale orange, and about double the size of a large room to a normal human. In its centre there was a grand piano, coloured a darker shade of orange. Jacob Crab was sitting on a very squat stool playing with the very tips of his giant claws. The Crab Gang from Zawn Cove were all gathered together on top of the piano. Jacob Crab's drab greenish colour had changed, almost as if he had changed clothes for his concert pianist performance. He was now bright electric blue, with pink and purple streaks.

Very faintly. Very, very faintly, Bibi was able to make out some of the notes of 'Happy Birthday to You'. She got to her feet thinking that clearly the WobbleGumph requires acoustic fine-tuning, and although Captain Jimmy was nowhere to be seen she was relieved to discover Jacob Crab and the Crab Gang. They all seemed completely relaxed and seemingly unaware of any danger.

'Love the new colours, very jazzy. Whose birthday is it? Is it yours? Happy birthday to you, Jacob Crab, happy birthday to you.'

Jacob Crab did a high five with Bibi and said, 'Yeah, boss.' 'Ouch!' Bibi rubbed her hand – high fives against giant crab claws hurt.

♬♪ 'Happy birthday to you ♬♪
♪ Squashed sand eels to stew ♬♪
♪ Lots of seaweed in the rockpool ♪
♬♪ Happy birthday to you,' ♬

sang the Crab Gang.

'Have you seen Captain Jimmy?' she asked Jacob Crab, anxiously glancing back over her shoulder towards the direction of the dark blue chamber, thinking that she felt a vibration or a ripple wave, worrying that she was being followed, fearful that she could get trapped before finding the way out.

'He's gettin' his cogs adjusted, he is,' Jacob Crab said, continuing to tinker on the piano in a nonsensical musical way.

'Cogs adjusted?' Bibi almost yelled but stifled it. 'What are they doing to him? Is it dangerous? Will it change him? Do they want control of his mind?' She was feeling frantic and could almost have burst into tears, but she was determined to be brave, save Captain Jimmy and find a way back to Zawn Cove. It was a strange thing, because although Captain Jimmy was plastic she felt very close to him, perhaps even loved him a bit (even though he was as daft as a loo brush, a thought that made her smile).

The thing was, she believed in Captain Jimmy. In a very strange and mysterious way she believed that his plastic heart was in the right place and that he, more than any of the others wanted the oceans clean and pure again. Lots of thoughts were whizzing around in her head. Could it be, she wondered (although it was a bit of a mad thought), that the mermaids had created Captain Jimmy but that he had become too good, too committed, too weirdly clever, and that the mermaids were jealous of him? Jealous of him brewing Horrid Green Custard, jealous of the *Ocean Flyer* that he had built, jealous of the fact the he had made flying boots and a flying collar – and finally, jealous of her, of Bibi and the fact that she was in many ways closer to Captain

Jimmy Ocean than they were? Had the mermaids created something that had taken on its own life, had now outgrown them and their undersea world, and could it be that they were now trying to regain control of their prodigy? If that was true then both she and Princess Liquorice were in more danger than she had ever imagined.

There was no way that the mermaids could ever allow them to escape from the maze of Colours in the WobbleGumph, and to be with Captain Jimmy in the World Above, at Zawn Cove, sailing in the *Ocean Flyer*, fighting off Oscar Shark Monster, having massive adventures away from mermaid control.

Jacob Crab interrupted her frantic line of thinking. 'That Izzy Brains, she says he needs a toopoozin jab to get his odd way of thinking sorted out. That's what she said when she and that Izzy Wonder and that Lavendoria took him off to the green-coloured Colour.'

Bibi's phone pinged with a message from OSM which read:

'Sticky buns sold out.'

Bibi shook her phone angrily: 'And I don't even have a signal down here! That's it, that's enough nonsense,' Bibi cried in her very determined stamping-her-foot-down way.

'Jacob Crab, I need your help. It could be that Captain Jimmy is in great danger of being normalised, perhaps we are all in danger one way or another, but we need to rescue Jimmy first. Are you with me?'

♬♪ 'We're the crew, how do you do ♬♪
♬ Which way's the rescue – just give us a clue ♬
♬♪ Captain Jimmy's cogs seemed alright to us ♪
♪ What's up with the mermaids, making such a fuss ♪
♬♪ Open a Colour close a Colour, easy to get lost ♬
♬ Down in '*the substance*' it's weird but at
least there's no frost ♬
♪ And why are doors called Colours here anyway? ♬♪
♬♪ It seems like a trick to confuse,
but we're on holiday, yeh!' ♪

sang the Crab Gang scampering round and round the orange chamber looking for an escape Colour to open.

Jacob Crab stopped playing the piano, turned slowly, looked at Bibi, lifted himself up on his eight brightly coloured legs and flexed his gaudy electric blue giant claws. 'Let's be getting to it,' he said in his very-less-than-awesome squeaky voice. 'Let's be getting our captain rescued.'

Princess Liquorice barked at the Colour and in less than a second divided by a second, the entire orange Colour was filled with all of the mermaids led by Lavendoria, moving gracefully upright, fluttering their broad mermaid tails as if in water – which, in one of its forms, the WobbleGumph or '*substance*' was.

'Found you at last,' sighed Izzy Peach, with a knowing and, Bibi thought, rather menacing flutter of her eyelashes.

The mermaids circled around Bibi and Princess Liquorice. Jacob Crab, behind the grand piano, opened and closed his great claws with a clacking sound, which, although partly deadened by the WobbleGumph, was still loud and scary.

Bibi, noticing that Izzy Brains was holding a hypodermic needle, picked up Princess Liquorice, who was growling and menacingly showing her teeth.

'We have such a wonderful surprise for you, darling Bibi,' Lavendoria said. 'We're all so excited and just know that you'll love it. Please be so good as to lead the way, Izzy Brains. And put the horrid needle away; we won't be needing that just at the moment.'

# - CHAPTER THIRTEEN -

## REAL AND UN-REAL

SnotTip was shaking when Bibi took the flexi ballpoint from her pocket.

'Can I just have a moment or two?' Bibi said to Lavendoria as she removed he backpack and took out the self-page-turning ship's logbook. 'So much wonderfully exciting stuff is happening that I would just like to make a few notes. I'm a really forgetful child and if I don't get things written down then they just fly right out of my head like butterflies. I won't keep you long, and then we can nip off and see this *wonderful surprise*. Won't be a jiffy.'

'Write fast, SnotTip,' Bibi hissed while pretending to suck on the ballpoint, 'and make sure that you write what I want and not what you want, *clear?*'

For the first time ever, SnotTip behaved and wrote everything Bibi guided the ballpoint to write. Bibi could feel that SnotTip was scared and she could see that the writing was shaky. Bibi wrote:

*This might or might not be true, but I believe that The Big Whizzo mermaids are holding me and Princess Liquorice prisoner and tampering with Captain Jimmy Ocean's plastic brain. It might be because they are jealous that their creation has outgrown them, leads a new life beyond their control and has new friends... or it might be something else.*

*A bit about The Big Whizzo for the World Above: All of the ocean-polluting plastic from all the world's oceans, it seems, is brought to this place by wind and currents. And here, in this undersea octo-recycling plant, the rubbish plastic is transformed into very mysterious pure white sand. The sand of this beach, from what I can make out, is like a stockpile, a sand store, ready to be made into something else. I'm not sure yet, but somehow I think that it's going to be mixed up with the Horrid Green Custard to make something else... something to dissolve or eat polluting plastic, or even convert it into something else... something useful and not harmful to marine creatures, perhaps. But I'm not exactly sure about that, it's just me trying to piece things together from the bits I hear from the mermaids and from Captain Jimmy.*

*And one more thing: It might be that it's not just Princess*

*Liquorice and me that are being held prisoner, because they do seem to know a lot about Granny Bluebell, and they do have sticky buns and sausage rolls so I'm wondering if she has been captured too. These mermaids do seem to have extraordinary powers, powers that are both scary and awesome, so I have to be careful and won't be able to write much more. They might even be able to know what I'm writing, although at the moment they're all leaning over the piano listening to Jacob Crab playing. I think that Jacob Crab is entertaining them to draw their attention away from me but I can't be sure, I can't be sure about anything.*

*Later I'll find a small container to seal these pages in and I'll attach it to Princess Liquorice's collar and hope that she'll be able to fly all the way home with this message.*

*Oh, the location here is The Big Whizzo, Ocean Beyond, Planet Earth, where all of the world's horrible thrown-away plastic bits gather together in one whizzy place.*

*PS. Perhaps the mermaids have found the solution to plastic pollution and I'm just being mean to them. Let's hope so.*

*PPS. Love you, Mum and Dad. Keep well and I hope I'll make it back for tea. Kisses.*

*This is true and signed by Bibi Lopez-Miller, aged 11, of Playing Place Cove, and verified by Princess Liquorice's*

*paw print and by SnotTip (who is not so bad really.)*
*circling in green congealed HGC.*

But SnotTip was not finished. SnotTip wrote, '*Go to Granny Bluebells, NOW!*'

'Finished,' Bibi called out across the orange Colour, and to Princess Liquorice she whispered, 'When you get a chance, fly off to the outer whizzing water wall and find a small container with a screw top, but not too small. I want to put a message inside. We can't do anything just at the moment to find Captain Jimmy, not with all of these mermaids around, but we'll just go along with what they want and await our opportunity. Okay? They're coming now, so watch out.'

The Colour was florescent pink and although it did not have a door (unlike the other Colour chambers that came and went like large expanding and contracting bubbles in jelly) it did creak. And it creaked in such a way that made Princess Liquorice cock her head and twitch her ears. It was a creak that she knew very well; but how could it be that the creak was down here, Princess Liquorice asked herself. And how could anything creak in the WobbleGumph because it mostly deadened sounds like creaks and musical notes.

Lavendoria took hold of Bibi's hand. Bibi flinched and

wanted to take her hand away. Lavendoria's hand was cold and fishy slippery, and also Bibi was trying to delay, waiting for Jacob Crab and the Crab Gang from Zawn Cove to catch up. She glanced everywhere, making a mental note of every single detail, as well as looking for a possible escape route once they had Captain Jimmy.

But Lavendoria held onto her hand tightly, insistently.

'Well, daughter of a marine biologist and wildlife photographer, believer in peculiar magic, wild adventures with a plastic sailor, a giant crab and singing crabs, a close friend of a talking, flying dog, a linguist and very smart for your age. Perhaps this will not amaze you as much as I expect it to,' Lavendoria said, in a rather creepily languid way.

And then there was a Granny Bluebell's door 'DING'. A cold shiver ran right through Bibi. Lavendoria turned, shook her tresses, smiled knowingly and tugged at Bibi's hand but Bibi's feet were glued to the spot. Her mind was racing. Was there another way out, she was desperately thinking. She glanced down at Princess Liquorice and nodded to her to fly up so that she could whisper in her ear. 'Nip her fin,' she hissed between closed teeth. Princess Liquorice was glad to oblige.

'Oh, that bad doggie's at it again!' Lavendoria cried, letting go of Bibi's hand and shooing Princess Liquorice away. Bibi turned, determined to make a dash out through the Colours and hope for the best, hope that Princess Liquorice's nose could sniff out where Captain Jimmy was being held '*captive*'.

As she turned on her heels, a wall of mermaids, all of the Izzys, appeared, forming a mermaid wall blocking her way. Bibi did not like the way that they were smiling at all but she had no choice but to turn back to where Lavendoria was waiting in front of the florescent pink Colour.

Lavendoria pushed the Colour open further. 'What can you smell, naughty doggie?' she asked Princess Liquorice while flipping to one side to be sure to be clear of nipping doggie teeth.

Princess Liquorice's nose twitched, and then she growled, and then she barked and then she flew forwards into the florescent pink Colour with the full force of a collar-propelled rocket.

'Sausage rolls,' she yelped, 'sausage rolls, wolf, wolf, wolf.'

Bibi followed, with all of the Izzys and Lavendoria close behind. This Colour was different to the other Colour bubbles. This Colour was like being inside a massive, wobbly out of focus jellyfish. There were shapes but nothing was clear. Bibi said, in a hushed voice 'what do you make of this, Liqcs?'

'Too busy sniffing,' Princess Liquorice whispered back.

'Why are you whispering?' Bibi whispered.

'Because you're whispering,' Princess Liquorice whispered.

'Stop it, you're being daft, Oh my dog! Look at that,' Bibi gasped in a half silent gasp.

Shapes began to form. First there was Granny Bluebell's old-fashioned cash register with its drawer at the bottom where the money was kept. And then, Granny Bluebell's faded red serving counter emerged from the swirling translucent jelly-like WobbleGumph.

'Very weird,' Princess Liquorice growled.

'Weirder than weird but it can't be a real shop it must be a dream,' Bibi said taking a smaller step forwards.

'Well the sniffers are good,' Liqcs growled under her breath.

'And what exactly are 'sniffers?' Bibi enquired, not exactly that bothered as she had more important things on her like mind like - was this a trap?

'Well sniffers are sniffers, of course, things that you sniff, like warm sausage roll sniffers,' Princess Liquorice was sniffing this way and that to locate the main sniffer source.

Other shop-like objects were slowly emerging from the translucent jelly; two glass display cases standing on the counter, for instance, one containing sticky buns and the other warm sausage rolls. And then, further back, row upon row, shelf upon shelf, of glass sweet jars, but not filled with sweets as you would expect, but filled with what looked like small green pebbles that were vibrating and jumping around inside of the jars.

Bibi cautiously edged forwards to inspect the jars more closely and as she did so, hardly having moved half a step, she jumped right out of her skin. 'Jimmy!' she cried. 'Jimmy, what have they done to you?'

Captain Jimmy leapt up from behind the counter wearing Granny Bluebell's floral pinny.

'Sticky buns for anyone?' he said grinning, 'I have sausage rolls as well....and all at deeply reduced undersea prices.'

Bibi rushed forwards, lent over the counter, grabbed him by the arms, pulled him towards her, kissed his cheek and urgently asked in a hushed whisper: 'Are you alright, what's been happening, have they given you a toopoozin injection yet?'

'Lots of today is stonking good but some is not – sticky buns to be eaten with care of the dentals,' Captain Jimmy stared Bibi straight in the eye and emphasized: '*Care of the dentals.*'

SnotTip wriggled to escape from Bibi's pocket. 'Oh, what is it now?' Bibi was more interested in trying to figure out if Captain Jimmy had been altered in any way. He looked the same she had to admit, but of course it was not the outside that mattered – it was the thinking bit in his head. She was a bit reluctant to use the word *'brain'* even to herself, so she stuck with *thinking bit* for the moment.

But SnotTip would not give up. 'So, what's your problem?' Still looking at Jimmy she took SnotTip out and held the ballpoint firmly in her closed hand which was resting on Granny Bluebell's 'replica' or whatever it was glass counter.

SnotTip managed to wriggle out between her fingers and write on a 'replica or whatever' notepad which Granny Bluebell used for adding up cake and sweet bills. SnotTip wrote: *'Beware!!!! Don't eat the note!!!!!'*

Bibi looked at the sticky bun that she had just picked up with her non-SnotTip hand, looked at Captain Jimmy, glanced over her shoulder at the mermaids who were smiling as if they were hiding a secret, and then took a small bite of the bun. With the tip of her tongue she felt paper, or something very like it.

To distract the mermaids, Bibi asked Captain Jimmy: 'What exactly are those jumping green-ish things in the sweet jars behind you on the shelves?'

'Oh, yes, that's alright if you like that sort of thing,' Captain Jimmy replied evasively. 'Take a closer look from around this side of the counter. Why don't you do that?

NOW would be an excellent moment,' he finished by speaking abruptly and fixing Bibi with as steely a gaze as plastic can manage.

And then on perfect distracting cue, probably prompted by Jacob Crab who was muscling in through the shop doorway and causing the bell to ding, ding, ding, the Crab Gang sang:

♬♪ How many teeth do you need to bite? ♪
♪ Granny Bluebell thinks three's alright ♪
♪ The Crab Gang love lollies to nibble and suck ♪
♪ Stinking seaweed flavour if you're really in luck ♪
♪But down in the shop beneath the waves ♪
♪ A peculiar thing is invented that saves ♪
♪There are octopus creatures working day and night ♪
♬ For a really strange shop that is out of sight ♪
♪And what they have made out of plastic and bits,♪
♪ Horrid Green Custard, special secrets and nits ♪
♪ Are jars full of pebbles that jump ♪
♪ Packed with microbes, it's said, and magic
and gump ♩♪

Captain Jimmy laughed. Lavendoria laughed. All of the seven Izzys laughed. Even Jacob Crab laughed, although he had no idea what exactly he was laughing about. The undersea version of Granny Bluebell's shop had now fully formed out of the translucent jelly-like stuff, but looking through the open doorway into what was, in the Playing Place Cove version of the shop, Granny Bluebell's back parlour, it was still bluish jelly-like.

While the Crab Gang sang, Bibi slipped around the end of the counter and beside Captain Jimmy. She had nibbled the note from out of the sticky bun. It was a bit sticky and crumby but she un-scrunched it, turned it one way then the other only to see that it was blank. 'This is one of your funny notes, isn't it, one that you forgot to write, so what was meant to be on it? Quick tell me, while the mermaids are helping Jacob Crab squeeze through the doorway.'

SnotTip was still in her hand and started wriggling again. Bibi flattened the note out and let SnotTip write. The ballpoint wrote with spell binding speed:

*The mermaids want to make a MK II version of me. Izzy Brains is behind the plan with the help of Prof Gilbert Octopus who does mostly what he's ordered to do. The mermaids, or at least some of them, say that I a have a severe plastic-autistic spectrum disorder and that the new Plastic Jimmy II model will not have that flaw. I think that they want a Plastic Jimmy that they have more control over. Ha, Ha, what did they expect when they created a Jimmy Plastic genius? Ha, ha, ha! It could be that they're just scared of the plastic genius nutcase that they've created been to save the ocean who has taken on a life of his own. What do you know? What do they know? Yo! Now they want to get me munched up by the octo-recyclers. I need to escape before I'm toopoozined and doped down. I don't know how many of the other mermaids are in on the plot but too dangerous to stay here to find out. We can escape back to Ocean Flyer using your magic flying boots, flying in boot tandem. Jacob Crab will cover our escape and join us with the Crab Gang when we are ready just-in-time-to-sail, reverse whizz spiral up out of The Big Whizzo. We need to be ultra alert and ready to act as soon as the chance presents itself, which could be any moment from last week. Be aware that the Fatal Stinging Jellies, the FSJ, global ocean police, and particularly Inspector StingRay, have been alerted to seal all ports of exit and to do facial recognition check for any known criminal plastic person helpers. Are you my brave friend? Can you help? SnotTip is with us. YEH!!!!'*

Out of sight of the mermaids, Bibi squeezed Captain Jimmy's hand and whispered in his *genius's* plastic ear, 'It's what I thought, you can rely on Liqcs and me, no probs.'

With Jacob Crab eased through the Granny Bluebell's

shop doorway, Lavendoria turned and beckoned to Bibi with a twitchy finger motion and an I-have-a-secret-to-tell sort of wink.

Bibi was not so sure about what to do but Captain Jimmy nudged her. 'Go, we'll go together. Now is not the moment for the moon to wane outside of the orbit of Saturn. But stick together.'

'Why don't you stay and serve in the shop, Plastic Jimmy? Izzy Brains suggested, still gripping the toopoozin hypodermic, which in Bibi's eyes was frighteningly bigger, in an iron-like mad doctor mermaid grip. There might be a great rush of octopus customers for sticky buns, who knows?' and all of the Izzys and Lavendoria shook with laughter.

'I would like Captain Jimmy to come with me,' Bibi said defiantly. 'After all, his funny way of talking and his mad screwy thinking, is outrageous – I just can't get enough of hearing it, it's so awesomely crazy. C'mon, Plastic Jimmy Captain. Let's go and see what wonderful secrets Lavendoria has to show us in Granny Bluebell's undersea back parlour. And I think that you should take off the granny pinny. It's not very sea captain-ish. Okay, Lavendoria, lead the way.'

It was indeed an awesome secret that Lavendoria had to show. Bibi was amazed with herself. Amazed at her reaction to seeing row upon row of half-lifesize mermaids working with what appeared to be scientific instruments. Row upon row of them extending into the jelly distance. She laughed, Lavendoria laughed, all of the Izzys laughed with the exception of Izzy Brains who appeared to Bibi to be more focused on getting between her and Captain Jimmy than on anything else.

'I think that my mind has become sort of like a balloon that can be many shapes and sizes...' Bibi said, amazed by her own flexibility of thinking and her capacity to be just plain daft like Captain Jimmy was most of the time.

'Write this down in the ship's logbook purple section,' she ordered SnotTip, taking the logbook from her backpack. The pages opened in exactly the right place and SnotTip wrote more or less as instructed:

*Just visited Granny Bluebell's undersea shop and seen shelves of dancing pale green pebbles in jars but not yet sure what they are. Now in some sort of pink, glowing jelly-filled balloon laboratory filled with row upon row of white-coated MiniMermaid lab assistants. They work like mad for five minutes and then stop to laugh in unison for no apparent reason at all...*

Bibi's smartphone rang. 'Yes, Mum. No, I'm not in a pub drinking lemonade. You can hear wild laughter? I think that it must be the sound of the waves or something – maybe interference. Yes, I'm fine. No probs. Sorry bad line, bye, love you, bye, bye.'

While Bibi was on the phone, SnotTip wrote: *Captain Jimmy likes April Fool's jokes in June.*

Bibi returned the logbook to her backpack and tied a knot in SnotTip without reading what the ballpoint had written. SnotTip wriggled but to no avail as Bibi's attention was focused on the MiniMermaid laughing lab assistants who were also standing on their tails, clapping hands and chanting, '*Viva Plastic Jimmy, Plastic Jimmy for President!*'

Bibi started to join in the chant, but then it stopped mid *Presi...* and the mini lab assistants immediately became fixated on work.

Bibi turned to rib Captain Jimmy about his MiniMermaid fans but instead, out of the corner of her eye spotted the hypodermic syringe ready to jab downwards and shouldered Izzy Brains hard onto her back.

The whole laboratory shuddered and wobbled. Everyone in the laboratory froze and wobbled in their positions. And then it stopped. The shudder was no more. It was as if the shudder had never happened, as if it was an illusion of a shudder that was immediately forgotten.

Bibi helped Izzy Brains back on to her fin, brushed her scales down and apologised for *losing her balance* and knocking her over. While Izzy Brains was gathering herself by giving herself a good shimmy, Bibi took the opportunity to kick the fallen syringe beneath one of the lab tables and out of sight.

'So why was everyone laughing?' Bibi asked, taking Izzy Brain's hand and leading her away. She could see Izzy Brain's eyes looking this way and that on the floor beneath the lab benches.

'Everyone is laughing because they're laughing,' Captain Jimmy seemed genuinely bemused. 'Is a laughing reason necessary?'

'Well YES! Normally, YES! But, silly me, that's another world!'

'Follow me if you would kindly enjoy it.' Captain Jimmy led the way between the benches. Bibi still had Izzy Brains in tow and was gripping her cold fishy wriggly hand firmly. 'This is the very laboratory of vibrating mixing where inventions are very especially invented and Horrid Green Custard is vitally esteemed.'

'Where the dancing stones are invented, the ones in the sweet jars? Are they also made here?' Bibi was pleased with herself; she was getting into the swing of flexible thinking and even appeared to be asking the right flexible normal questions. But her attention slipped and so did her grip and Izzy Brains wriggled free.

Princess Liquorice was circling overhead, Bibi whistled to her to come: 'Follow her, the Brains one, follow her, she's after the big needle, see if you can find it first, pick it up and bring it here, but be careful, don't bite it hard, soft mouth remember, it's full of toopoozin which sounds pretty horrible and might be very dangerous for a dog. It's under the nearest table to the Granny Bluebell dinging door.'

Bibi felt another wobble-shudder. She looked around at the mermaid Izzy bosses, at the MiniMermaid lab assistants and finally at Captain Jimmy, but no one else appeared to notice anything. Princess Liquorice had zoomed off into the distant pink gel.

Captain Jimmy jumped up onto a workbench beside an enormously complicated machine made of twisted plastic tubes of all colours, miniature escalators going this way and that and a flop-juice converter of massive proportions. The MiniMermaids clapped. He bowed and then curtsied.

'Here is what we see with eyeballs stretched Horrid Green Custard supply dripping down from the barrels above into the High Speed Rotating Gloop Tube, along and up and around within the Gloop Bypass Interrupter, over and inside the Solid Gloop Intensifier, around the Basic Big Bend (BBB,) into the Mixed Microbe Ingester. Microbes are what matter, microbes perfectionly perfected and perfectionly engineered by the perfectionly perfect MiniMermaids.' All of the MiniMermaids clapped and hooted and Jacob Crab clacked his claws loudly.

The Izzy Boss Mermaids were less impressed and forced some very forced smiles, while in the pink distance haze Izzy Brains was searching beneath benches just as Princess Liquorice was heading back to Bibi with the syringe in her mouth. There was yet another shudder, the biggest jarring shudder vibration of all.

# - CHAPTER FOURTEEN -

## AND NOW THIS! WHAT A MESS!

Izzy Brains spotted Princess Liquorice with the toopoozin-filled hypodermic needle in her mouth flying back towards Captain Jimmy and Bibi. She leapt up and gave chase, swimming fast with her strong fin churning the WobbleGumph.

'Behind you, Liqcs!' Bibi shouted. 'She's behind you! Don't lark about doing barrel rolls. Go faster. She's gaining...*faster!*'

Princess Liquorice was unable to hear Bibi but growled in excitement when she saw her waving her arms wildly, thinking it was probably a new game and started a fun loop-the-loop when, as she turned, she caught sight of the angry mermaid zooming up on her, eyes bulging and looking horribly mean.

No chance of catching me, Princess Liquorice thought to herself, giving a chuckling low growl. She spiralled down towards the rows of MiniMermaids and whizzed under a bench and out the other side, catching Izzy Brains totally by surprise, appearing behind her and touching her tail with her whiskers.

'You wait, you annoying little creature, just you wait!' Izzy Brains cried, but before she could do anything there was another more prolonged vibration. This vibration caused a ripple to pulsate along the pink gel WobbleGumph that shook Princess Liquorice and caused the hypodermic syringe to fall from her mouth.

Bibi saw it spinning and gasped with trepidation at what would happen if it smashed. Izzy Brains made a dive to catch it but it was bouncing along the rippling, vibrating pink gel WobbleGumph of Granny Bluebell's inner parlour laboratory and she missed it.

It was the time for the MiniMermaids to laugh, so they all laughed together and then got back to work.

'Jimmy catch it!' Bibi cried, lifting him up using magic flying boot power, but it rippled along the rippling gel just out of his reach. Princess Liquorice zoomed in, but just as she was about to soft mouth grab it, it flipped over so the needle end was pointing straight at her mouth, and she yelped and dived beneath it, but, but, but... Izzy Brains, who had been swimming right behind Princess Liquorice, right on her tail, almost touching it, had no time to dive, no time to get out of the way, no time to avoid the sharp hypodermic needle point which stuck right into the end of her nose.

It was time to laugh again and all of the MiniMermaids laughed. Izzy Brains tried to stop but was unable to stop. She tried to stop swimming but had too much momentum and crashed nose first into the High Speed Rotating Gloop Tube. It shattered into a total mess of flying green gloop globules, covering everything and everybody, totally encasing Izzy Brains (who was at the same time turning deep purple with a heavy overdose of toopoozin right into her nose).

The Izzys spluttered and gasped with shock. The MiniMermaids laughed again because it was laughing time.

Professor Gilbert Octopus, wiping gloop from his eyes and helping Captain Jimmy to his feet said: 'It might take a while to fix.'

'I'll do a just-in-time temporary job which will have it up and running by the year before last,' Captain Jimmy laughed punching what he called '*the substance*'.

Jacob Crab discovered that he rather liked the taste of the green gloop and was sucking dollops off Izzy Brains who was completely covered.

'Look, Jimmy, look!' Bibi gasped. 'Izzy Brains is shrinking. Is that because Jacob Crab? No, it can't be... But look, she is, she really is.'

As they watched, she shrank to the size of the MiniMermaids, and not only that, she moved to an empty place in front of a microscope and settled down to work. When the next MiniMermaid's time to laugh came, she laughed as well even though she was still deep purple coloured and looked very odd.

Prof Gilbert Octopus offered Bibi a tentacle and she shook it and smiled even though the ghastly suckered feel was not at all to her liking.

'Are you in charge?' she asked.

Prof Gilbert Octopus, Chief Marine Scientist of the factory that transforms plasticky bits, at your service,' he replied.

'Well, perhaps you could answer these questions: why is there a Granny Bluebell's down here, and has she been kidnapped and forced to reveal the recipe for sticky buns...?'

'And sausage rolls,' chipped in Princess Liquorice.

'Yes, and sausage rolls... Well, those are the questions that I would like answered, because kidnapping of old people is a very serious business you know. So, what have you got to say because there are some very weird things happening down here... Just look at the toopoozin incident, which it appears was intended to shrink Captain Jimmy. To mention just one of many, very many madcap happenings.

Answers please, and be ready to take notes, SnotTip.'

'Well my dear...' the Prof began, but Bibi stopped him.

'I would like straight and clear answers,' she demanded. 'Yes or no, has Granny Bluebell been kidnapped, yes or no?'

'Not at all,' replied Professor Gilbert Octopus turning to Captain Jimmy for confirmation.

'The shop's a replica. I dreamt it out of a mountain of zany thoughts that failed to evaporate in time,' Captain Jimmy replied.

'So, she's not here? She's not been harmed and you have discovered all of these baking secrets unaided by years of experience? Bibi questioned, not at all convinced.

'Have you got all of that down, SnotTip, verbatim; that is, every word written down? Bibi glanced at the page before going on to other questions that she urgently needed replies to. SnotTip had it all down, not in the neatest writing but it was just legible. But the ballpoint had also written at the end – *Don't forget OSM*.'

But then it was laughing time again and for a few seconds everything stopped for laughing. Bibi noticed that the reduced in size Izzy Brains was laughing louder and with more enthusiasm than any of the other MiniMermaids. 'Weird effect that toopoozin has,' she thought, and then smiled to herself. What if Plastic Jimmy had been jabbed as intended and was halved in size and laughed when the clock said laugh? It was an image of him that really amused her.

'Are you thinking of doing laughing time?' Captain Jimmy asked, seeing her smiling.

'No, I was thinking about why you have jumping green pebbles in Granny Bluebell's sweet jars. If this was a true replica shop, then they should be filled with sugar lemons, gob stoppers or chocolate fudge etc, etc. Oh, and I was also thinking... will I be back for supper in time?' Bibi laughed.

All of the MiniMermaids turned and looked at her frowning – *it was not laughing time.*

'We are not yet perfect,' Prof Gilbert Octopus admitted with his sad droopy octo face on. 'Our plan is simple, our plan is to add our especially genetically engineered ZooMicrobes, microbes that eat plastic and transform it into food suitable for sea creatures to safely eat and to add these ZooMicrobes to pebbles. The pebbles also contain Horrid Green Custard, which stimulates and feeds the microbes until they are placed on beaches. Beaches the world over. By our calculations one pebble per square kilometre of beach would be required. At first the ZooMicrobes feed off the Horrid Green Custard in the pebble and then leach into beach garbage plastic, do their plastic-to-food conversion job, and also multiply trillions of times and spread throughout the oceans.

At the moment' the ZooMicrobes are over stimulated

and the pebbles dance around wasting energy. Our team of MiniMermaids are working night and day to solve the problem before Plastic Jimmy does the first ZooMicrobe field trials on plastic polluted beaches worldwide – will it solve the plastic pollution problem that is killing our oceans? Our dream is that it will.'

It was a laughing moment and all of the MiniMermaids stopped work to laugh.

'That's odd, why do they...'

'To increase their fun intake, the joy quota, of course. Isn't it regulatory everywhere in this modern world? I am surprised,' exclaimed Prof Gilbert Octopus, a bit taken aback by Bibi's question.

The next vibration was more like a small shockwave. Even the MiniMermaids juddered at their benches and, for a moment, had to hold on to their instruments to prevent them falling to the floor.

Bibi looked at Captain Jimmy. 'That feels ominous to me,' she said.

Captain Jimmy said airily: 'It's the realignment of forces that refuse to be elastic.'

Professor Gilbert Octopus was still rattling on about ZooMicrobes have amazing powers to transform really nasty things into really nice useful, ocean saving things... Bibi interrupted him. 'Excuse me, Professor, but that tremor that just rattled everything about, in fact there have been a few, I don't know if you've noticed. They seem to be getting worse, and I wondered... Would you, in a scientific way, consider it anything to worry about? I have to admit, it does worry me. After all, an earthquake down here might be... well, to put it mildly... it would be sort of catastrophically cataclysmic, wouldn't it? I mean like, being down under the ocean would be super dodgy if you ask me, certainly for Liqcs and me, and Captain Jimmy too, I imagine.'

Prof Gilbert Octopus scratched his head with a sucker and looked puzzled. 'It could be...' he started to say, but was interrupted by the laughing moment and appeared to lose his train of thought.

'Can these ZooMicrobe thingies transform garbage plastic into yummy cheesy nibbles?' Princess Liquorice flew down, stuck her wet nose against Prof Gilbert's wet nose and asked.

'Excellent question, little dog, and the answer to that excellent question is, not as yet. Our focus at the moment is not cheesy nibbles but to find an efficient way to get microbes to transform garbage plastic into edible fish food.'

Bibi's phone tinged with a text, she glanced at it, gasped in horror and showed it to Prof Gilbert Octopus – *there was a short repeating video of an open shark's mouth with the letters OSM emerging from between rows of very sharp teeth.*

Composing herself, Bibi asked the Prof, 'does plastic, when swallowed, turn otherwise friendly marine creatures into hideous, ferocious monsters......and, and...is it possible that they have smartphones?'

The MiniMermaids had a laughing moment but this time Professor Gilbert joined in laughing. He laughed like a wobbling purple jelly. 'Yes to the first question, we have evidence that toxic plastic can cause marine mutations... and a definite NO, NO, NO to the second. Marine mammals with smartphones, now that would be sensational!'

'So how do you explain that video, that shark mouth, those teeth, that OSM business... how do you explain that?' Bibi demanded, becoming very insistent, more out of fear than anger, what with the tremors and shockwaves, and now a shark video on her phone... Well, there was scary and there was scary, but it was all getting awesomely out-of-hand scary and she wanted answers.

But before Prof Gilbert could reply, her phone rang again 'Oh drat!' she exclaimed, but it was not the shark this time.

'Hi, Mum. Yes, we're having a great time. Back soon, love you. Licky kisses from Liqcs... Sorry you're breaking up, better go now. Bye.'

# - CHAPTER FIFTEEN -

## SMARTPHONES AND SHARKS

Jacob Crab, totally bloated with green gloop, wiped his mouth with the back of his giant claw, burped loudly and crabbed sideways to get a closer look at the screen. The Crab Gang scuttled up onto Jacob Crab's carapace. The Boss Mermaids all gathered and, when they had finished laughing time, the nearest benches of MiniMermaids moved closer, but not the reduced Izzy Brains, who had now become a workaholic.

Bibi replayed the shark mouth video with the OSM words between his teeth. 'So, what about that?' Bibi questioned.

♬♪ 'Is that Oscar Shark Monster that we see? ♪
♪ What, is he a famous movie star – no that can't be? ♬
♬♪ We don't like the look of those very sharp teeth ♬♪
♬ ♪It could be that he's not even flossed beneath ♪

♬ But of course if he really is famous and
wants a band ♪
♪ Don't forget us – for payment, a seaweed
sandwich will be grand ♪
♬♪...and a play in the sand,' ♬♪

sang the Crab Gang from Zawn Cove.

Professor Gilbert Octopus took hold of the smartphone, wrapped a slimy tentacle around it and held the screen very close to one bulging eye and laughed.

Lavendoria was next to take a closer look, and Bibi played the video again so that she could take all of the shark's full-frontal mouth detail in as she scrutinised it closely.

'That's so good, we love that don't we, girls?' exclaimed Lavendoria. 'What a pity that Izzy Brains has *downsized*,' and all of the remaining Izzys laughed.

'I find it scary, terrifying even, and all you lot can do is laugh,' Bibi was a bit taken aback by their reaction. 'Captain Jimmy, what do you think? Remember that this was very, very mysteriously sent to my phone, my phone deep in the ocean, my phone down in The Big Whizzo, my phone down in The Big Whizzo with a shark the size of an island lurking somewhere around the rim. *Lurking...*' she emphasized.

Bibi played the video for a fourth time. Captain Jimmy took a small mirror from his pocket and watched it in the mirror. While he was adjusting the angle, there was another small judder. Enough to move a pair of white lab gloves and reveal the newly refilled toopoozin needle that had been covered up and was now close to where Izzy H20 was resting her hand.

'Exactly!' Captain Jimmy sighed when he had the adjustment to his exact satisfaction.

'Exactly what?' Bibi demanded feeling double or even treble exasperated and with a corner of her mind concerned about the hypodermic and whether the Mermaid Bosses were going to have another go at jabbing Jimmy.

And then the MiniMermaids started a laughing break.

'Stop!' shouted Bibi. 'Are you all mad? Something terrible is about to happen any second and all you can do is laugh and never answer a straight question. What is wrong with you?'

Bibi turned again to Captain Jimmy: 'What does it mean, what does this OSM video mean. You must know, in your weird plastic genius way you are meant to know everything. Don't you?'

'Yes!' cried Captain Jimmy.

'Pure genius,' exclaimed Prof Gilbert Octopus.

'Izzy Brains was wrong about you Plastic Jimmy, your

brain cogs have cunning built in,' Lavendoria said haughtily, as if she had known it all along, and never believed one word, not one single word, that Brains had said against Jimmy. Out of the corner of her eye, Bibi spotted that Lavendoria gave a small nod to Izzy $H_2O$.

'I hope we're not going to celebrate with a green gloop toast, I'm full to the eyeballs,' groaned Jacob Crab.

♪ 'Now Jimmy's the star, hurrah, hurrah ♬
♬ Not that we know what sort of star you are ♪
♬ Of course we believe and that's what matters ♪
♪ Izzy Brains was wrong that his cogs were in tatters,' ♪

sang the Crab Gang from Zawn Cove.

'Is this some sort of pantomime?' Bibi cried, almost in tears of frustration. 'Your whole world, this amazing world, this Big Whizzo, this octo-recycling, this totally bizarre replica Granny Bluebell's, this pink jelly lab filled with MiniMermaid lab assistants who have laughing fits, that you have created to save the oceans from being destroyed by polluting plastic, is itself about to be shaken apart by earth tremors that are getting stronger and stronger. There might be another Big Whizzo crushing one any second – and all that you all do about it... is, is... to talk gibberish. I cannot believe it!'

It was amazing to see an octopus do a roly-poly in a tangle of his tentacles and floppy body. It made Bibi gasp and clap with delight and even though it was not official laughing time, the MiniMermaids laughed anyway at the Prof's wild antics.

'Ha, ha! Yes, Jimmy you were right,' he laughed with a slippery black inky laugh as he straightened himself up and attempted to regain his professorial composure. 'She's the one alright, very smart of you to pick the daughter of a marine biologist, perfect, just perfect!'

'*Perfect for what*?' Bibi demanded. 'I'm not a sandwich you know; just perfect to be eaten. I'm not even a sticky bun, which is even more perfect to be eaten... And I am certainly not perfect to be shrunk with a toopoozin injection and nor is Captain Jimmy, so there. And look at this. What about this?' Bibi pushed the smartphone right against his eye.

'Yes, I see. I'm not short-sighted, you know. I can see OSM very clearly – *Ocean Shore Miracle*.' Prof Gilbert Octopus replied with a sort of wobbly shrug. 'Did you think that it had another meaning?'

Bibi was totally gobsmacked. She turned the phone around and stared at the image, played the video and stared at it – she had totally convinced herself that OSM was Oscar Shark Monster not... 'What was that you said,

Ocean Shore Miracle? What's that when it's at home, anyway?'

Captain Jimmy gave Bibi a playful nudge. 'It's one of my effervescent of bubbles bouncing upwards and out and bursting on your tongue angel dust ideas,' Captain Jimmy laughed. 'Ocean Shore Miracle is just a jobbing, bobbing, working title with might be changed last winter but for now it is where your involvement will be cutting edge.'

'Ok... fascinating... And it has absolutely nothing to do with Oscar Shark Monster or with the risk of us all being eaten alive?' Bibi was yet to be totally convinced that this was not some trick, game or scam, and she still had half an eye on the protruding needle that no mermaid had yet bothered to cover up with the surgical gloves.

'No, absolutely none,' Professor Gilbert Octopus, said reassuringly. 'That poor old, toxic plastic-poisoned and probably terribly mutated Oscar Shark is hundreds of miles away by now – but, and this is very hush-hush. We do have a MiniMermaid section working on an antidote to the toxicity in his blood which is causing the abnormal growth and unpredictable anger, but, like I said, very hush-hush.'

'Ok, so I was wrong,' Bibi conceded. 'It's true that there are times when my imagination does run a bit wild, I admit that, but answer this: why have I been receiving these OSM messages on my phone. I mean, how do they get there? Who has my number? Do you have my number? Does Captain Jimmy have my number? And anyway, he doesn't even have a phone himself to send them, does he?'

'A computer glitch, some telecommunications error, some mix up with lines of geo-nodal waves, I'll get the tech boys to look into it. But the fact is, nothing to worry about from the jolly old shark. Much more importantly, we have found you.' Gilbert reassured.

'Well, that's that sorted, I suppose. And what's this other thing, this Ocean Shore Miracle and me being involved and it being cutting edge, whatever that exactly means, and what do you mean that you've *found me?*'

'Dreams are dreams and fiddly-de-de, yes, I found you clever me and I'm climbing up a prickly gum tree the better to see,' Captain Jimmy sang while dancing round and round in a tight circle. 'The long and the tall of it is that we need your help. When you grow bigger upwards to human size and then being clever and universitied, you will be our up-surface rep. human-bodied scientific spokesperson up going. We...'

But before he could say more, Granny Bluebell's replica cake shop oven door suddenly flew open and a tray of sticky buns fell onto the floor as the whole Big Whizzo undersea cavern trembled with a terrible tremble.

Microscopes shuddered, Professor Gilbert hung on

by his tentacles and all of the mermaid scientists gulped bubbles of disbelief into the WobbleGumph.

Next, the shop door of Granny Bluebell's replica shop suddenly burst off its hinges with a gloop and a gurgle and a ting-a-ling of the bell. A tooth ripped through the wall.

Jacob Crab tossed MiniMermaids this way and that, laughing as they tumbled over each other, over the benches, over the instruments and became entangled in the High Speed Rotating Gloop Tube that was in the process of being reassembled by a team of MiniMermaid mechanics in zany lime green overalls.

'Let me at 'im,' Jacob Crab was yelling in a high pitch squeak, 'I's sick of 'im being horrendous.'

Another tooth appeared and then another glistening and eerie in the pink glow of lab light that was pulsating and flickering as if any minute there would be a total power failure and blackout in depth. In The Big Whizzo depths of the quivering gel of Granny Bluebell's back parlour laboratory.

'I was right,' cried Bibi, and in the confusion, taking the opportunity to brush the hypodermic to the floor with her arm, stamped on it and smashed it to bits.

This was an emergency and SnotTip just leapt out of Bibi's pocket and wrote in big letters on Prof Gilbert's whiteboard: *PURPLE, PURPLE, SPREADING*, and then jumped back and hunkered down in her pocket.

Bibi glanced back. A cloud of purple toopoozin was rising up and slowly spreading out through the WobbleGumph pink gel.

'OMD!' she cried, 'Don't breathe – we'll be miniaturized. 'Liqcs, get out... Fly the other way.'

'What into the monster shark's mouth?' Princess Liquorice barked in alarm and confusion.

'Where are the Izzys?' Bibi said to herself, looking around and seeing that they were gone – and the MiniMermaids were all disappearing too – into the WobbleGumph, into nowhere, into another Colour she presumed.

Jacob Crab had his mighty shell against the bulging wall with his giant claws braced, but was bit by bit being pushed back as more and more teeth broke through.

Grabbing Prof Gilbert by a tentacle, Bibi started to pull him clear of the enveloping purple toopoozin that was slowly drifting forwards, threatening to envelop the entire parlour laboratory.

'Don't breathe it in, Prof. Hold your breath!' she cried as she pulled but she could see that it was already too late and Prof Gilbert was shrinking.

♩♪ 'All out, all out, run and scurry ♪
♬♪Let's get out of here in a hurry ♪
♪ We're mad with panic and worry ♪
♪ There's a monster mouth behind that tooth ♪
♪ Ready to crunch and gobble and swallow ♪
♪ So forget the rhyme... let's just GO,' ♪

squealed the Crab Gang from Zawn Cove as they madly scuttled into Granny Bluebell's waste bin in panic.

As Bibi pulled Prof Gilbert clear and he breathed in a few clear breaths of pure the WobbleGumph it appeared that his shrinking stabilized.

'That was a close call he gasped,' after a few more intakes of clean the WobbleGumph and even joked, 'well, I did need to lose a few kilos.'

Princess Liquorice was on Jacob Crab's carapace barking as wildly as it was possible for a small terrier dog to bark when confronted by the largest and angriest shark in the whole history of sharks.

Captain Jimmy Ocean, Plastic Jimmy on the other hand was sitting on one of the MiniMermaid lab benches in the lotus position very calmly staring into pink gel WobbleGumph space.

'Jimmy!' Bibi shouted, 'this is no time for Zen, we're about to get gobbled and Prof Gilbert has been diet-ed.'

Captain Jimmy was OMMMMM-ing away completely oblivious to the impending disaster.

As the front wall of Granny Bluebell's cake shop creaked and groaned, shook and vibrated and shuddered, jars of the magic Mermaid Stones fell from the shelves and smashed on the primrose yellow painted floor with the escaped stones dancing about with their super engineered, genetically re-arranged microbes – *danger activated* – bouncing out of control with diet-ified Prof Gilbert doing his best to calm the genetic zipping around.

Jacob Crab squeaked, 'He's got breath like a dinosaur that's been eating marinated rotten skunks doused in a thousand-island slime dressing… can't hold it… can't HOLDDDDD.'

'That's it!' Bibi shouted at the top of her voice. 'THAT. IS. IT. This adventure has gone far enough. Plastic cog-brained genius Captain Jimmy Ocean, stop playing games and get us out of here. NOW, right NOW!'

Captain Jimmy sprung out of his lotus position on the bench to a race ready starting crouch on the floor. 'This way,' he whispered mysteriously to Bibi who was very close. 'Come this way before tectonic plates reach Grand Prix speed.' Captain Jimmy grabbed Bibi's hand.

'Whistle to Princess Liquorice,' he said leaning towards Bibi ear, 'we only have seconds before there are none. Hold

Oscar back a few moments more and I'll be with you with a rescue, Jacob Crab.'

'Save Bibi Lopez-Miller,' Prof Gilbert Octopus called out.

'It's being done and at breathless speed,' Captain Jimmy shouted back while leading Bibi in around Granny Bluebell's serving counter and through a side door.

'This won't help!' Bibi screamed, alarmed that there was no back-door escape at Granny Bluebell's – not the Playing Place Cove *real-life* version anyway – there was only her baking oven.

'The oven, yes the oven!' cried Captain Jimmy,' his voice rising to a high pitch with excitement and awe. 'The oven, the glorious oven, the oven that bakes the Mermaid Stones to perfection beyond any perfection that a microbe could dream in their wildest dreams.'

'Jimmy,' Bibi protested, '*isn't this an emergency?*'

Emergency or not, Captain Jimmy stopped to open the oven door and let the jumping stone, microbe packed, Horrid Green Custard fuelled, Mermaid Stones out to dance and cool on the worn flagstone floor.

'The wall's going... can't...' came the desperate squeaky shout from Jacob Crab.

Princess Liquorice flew in barking like mad, 'Jimmy, Jimmy... he's through!'

♬♪ 'One tooth, two teeth, three and four ♩♪
♩♪ Gnashing, gashing coming through the door ♬♪
♬♪ Smashing the cake sign, tingling the bell ♩♪.........

and then the words trailed off.

Working frantically, Jimmy moved a pile of empty cardboard boxes to reveal a small door.

'That's the dumb waiter elevator thingy in the old hotel where the REAL Granny Bluebell's is in Playing Place Cove. It hasn't been used for yonks and yonks, and anyway this one might be an illusion and anyway. So what?' Bibi groaned dismissively.

'It goes up!' Jimmy shouted excitedly, it's been adapted by thought and thinking hard as was done when I was doing it on the bench sitting cross-legged with my plastic legs aching badly but with mind focused hard. Take off the flying boots and collar – we need them – Jacob Crab and I need then to escape back to the *Ocean Flyer* and to get out of The Big Whizzo quick, quick. Squeeze in hard and now, into the dumb waiter, elevator, lift going up small box- like space which will make rescue possible. Do it, do it!' Captain Jimmy was shouting and pushing and undoing Princess Liquorice's magic flying collar all in a mad flurry of movement.

'It only goes from the kitchen to the dining room in the

old hotel and it's just for food and dirty plates and it's really cramped and it works by pulling a rope which is probably really rotten and broken,' Bibi protested, thinking this is really mad and stupid but what other choice is there?

'Jimmy, I tell you this is just bonkers beyond belief,' Bibi said, sort of resigned to the madness and kicked off the magic boots that Captain Jimmy immediately slipped into.

'It goes up,' Jimmy insisted, 'Squeeze in quick. Go on, squeeze in.'

'It only goes to the dining room, I tell you...and that's if it's working at all. It's never used.'

'It goes up,' Jimmy kept insisting, while pushing Bibi and Princess Liqcs into the very small space where Bibi had to crouch right down to be squashed in.

'But what about you? What about Jacob Crab, what about the Crab Gang from...' Bibi was saying when...

Whoosh!

# - CHAPTER SIXTEEN -

## THE RETURN TO WHAT WAS

The first thing that Bibi noticed was that that the grass was damp and she had dew on her bare feet. Emerging from the 'dumb waiter', which was there and was not there at more or less the same instant, Princess Liquorice immediately dashed off chasing a rabbit without even the slightest thought of flying using her *magic flying collar* (which had been left behind with Captain Jimmy anyway.)

'So, he was right,' Bibi said to herself, her head spinning, feeling dazed, out of breath and awesomely disorientated. 'Wow! Yes, he was right. *It goes up*.'

Trying to gather her thoughts, she walked around The Old Lookout Tower as if she might find a clue, but a clue to what? That was the question. A clue to The Big Whizzo, a clue to Mermaid Stones, a toopoozin clue... Well, a clue to what?

'Wow!' she repeated again, as if it was the only word left